A HERO'S ADVENTURE

Theseus stopped. There was a huge brute of a man facing him. He was called Pityocamptes, which means "pine-bender." He said to Theseus, "Just hold this for a moment like a good fellow, will you?"

"Certainly," said Theseus.

Theseus grasped the pine tree, let his mind go dark and all his strength flow downward, anchoring him to the earth like a rock. Pityocamptes let go of the tree, expecting to see Theseus fly into the air. Nothing happened. The giant could not believe his eyes. He leaned his head closer to see. Then Theseus let go.

The tree snapped up, catching the giant under the chin, knocking him unconscious. Theseus bent the tree again, swiftly bound the giant's wrists to it. He pulled down another tree and tied Pityocamptes' legs to that . . . and then let both pines go. They sprang apart. Half of Pityocamptes hung from one tree, half from the other. Theseus wiped the pine tar from his hands and continued on his way.

For my wife, Dorothy

CONTENTS

INTRODUCTION

These were the first stories I ever heard. I was four years old, and my young uncle was practicing his Greek on me. He read me the *Iliad* and the *Odyssey,* translating as he went. The unknown words poured over me like dark music, and when he turned to English it was always a letdown. I was very glad to hear what was happening, and wanted to know what happened next— but still there seemed something missing, the golden hero voices, sea whispers, spear shock. I had been bitten by poetry in the dark, and didn't know it.

Later, modeling myself after my uncle, I studied Greek and Latin and read the stories the way Hesiod told them; and Herodotus, Homer, Vergil, Ovid . . . and knew the old enchantment. Then I went to them in most of their English versions, and again felt this terrible loss.

So I began to tell them myself.

What are they then, these stories so often retold?

In Greek mythology heroes and monsters alike are spawned by the gods. The Gorgons, those snake-haired horrors, are grand-daughters of Rhea, mother of Zeus, which makes them cousins of their arch-enemy, Perseus. In other words, both good and evil come from the gods. Good is the divine enemy expressing itself through men of high deeds. Evil is the same energy, twisted. When hero confronts monster in these myths it is apt to be a family quarrel.

This pagan idea has influenced all the religions that came after.

The birth of the monster is attended by rage, and that is what makes him monstrous, the wrath of a god—or, more often, a goddess—carving a dangerous, ugly form for itself out of living flesh.

These Greek myths are drenched in sunlight, and this sunlight is more than weather; it is a moral quality. Heroes love to cavort in the open air, to fly, to cleave the burning sea, race on the hills, hunt over the fields. But monsters belong to darkness. Where the Gorgons live it is always winter. Cerberus, the three-headed dog, guards the gate of dark Tartarus, the land of the dead. Scylla and Echidne, the dreaded serpent-women, lurk in a sea-cave waiting to swallow the tides, make ship-wrecks, catch sailors and crack their bones. The Minotaur howls in a maze of shadows. The monsters wait in darkness, and when heroes hunt them, they must come in out of the sun, and the ordeal starts right there.

So we see a great religious theme—the eternal struggle between the powers of Light and the powers of Darkness embodied in these simple stories in a way that has branded itself on man's consciousness forever.

BERNARD EVSLIN

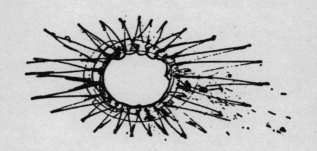

THE GODS

Zeus

Cronos, father of the gods, who gave his name to time, married his sister Rhea, goddess of earth. Now, Cronos had become king of the gods by killing his father, Uranus, the First One. The dying Uranus had prophesied, saying, "You murder me now and steal my throne—but one of your own sons will dethrone you, for crime begets crime."

So Cronos was very careful. One by one, he

swallowed his children as they were born. First three daughters—Hestia, Demeter, and Hera; then two sons—Hades and Poseidon. One by one, he swallowed them all.

Rhea was furious. She was determined that he should not eat her next child who she felt sure would be a son. When her time came, she crept down the slope of Olympus to a dark place to have her baby. It was a son, and she named him Zeus. She hung a golden cradle from the branches of an olive tree and put him to sleep there. Then she went back to the top of the mountain. She took a rock and wrapped it in swaddling clothes and held it to her breast, humming a lullaby. Cronos came snorting and bellowing out of his great bed, snatched the bundle from her and swallowed it, clothes and all.

Rhea stole down the mountainside to the swinging golden cradle and took her son down into the fields. She gave him to a shepherd family to raise, promising that their sheep would never be eaten by wolves.

Here Zeus grew to be a beautiful young boy, and Cronos, his father, knew nothing about him. Finally, however, Rhea became lonely for him and brought him back to the court of the gods, introducing him to Cronos as the new cupbearer. Cronos was pleased because the boy was beautiful.

One night Rhea and Zeus prepared a special drink. They mixed mustard and salt with the nectar. Next morning, after a mighty swallow, Cronos vomited up first a stone, and then Hestia, Demeter, Hera, Hades, and Poseidon—who, being gods, were still undigested, still alive. They thanked Zeus and immediately chose him to be their leader.

Then a mighty battle raged. Cronos was joined by the Titans, his half-brothers, huge, twisted, dark creatures taller than trees, whom he kept pent up in the mountains until there was fighting to be done. They attacked the young gods furiously. But Zeus had allies too. He had gone to darker caverns—caves under caves under caves, deep in the mountainside—formed by the first bubbles of the cooling earth. Here Cronos thousands of centuries before (a short time in the life of a god) had pent up other monsters, the one-eye Cyclopes and the Hundred-handed Ones. Zeus unshackled these ugly cousins and led them against the Titans.

There was a great rushing and tumult in the skies. The people on earth heard mighty thunder and saw mountains shatter. The earth quaked and tidal waves rolled as the gods fought. The Titans were tall as trees, and old Cronos was a crafty leader. He attacked fiercely, driving the young gods before him. But Zeus had laid a trap. Halfway up the slope of Olympus, he whistled for his cousins, the Hundred-handed Ones, who had been lying in ambush. They took up huge boulders, a hundred each, and hurled them downhill at the Titans. The Titans thought the mountain itself was falling on them. They broke ranks and fled.

The young goat-god Pan was shouting with joy. Later he said that it was his shout that made the Titans flee. That is where we get the word "panic."

Now the young gods climbed to Olympus, took over the castle, and Zeus became their king. No one knows what happened to Cronos and his Titans. But sometimes mountains still explode in fire and the earth still quakes, and no one knows exactly why.

Hera

Now, these gods reigned for some three thousand years. There were many of them, but twelve chief ones. Zeus married his sister Hera—a family habit. They were always quarreling. He angered her by his infidelities; she enraged him with her suspicions. She was the queen of intriguers and always found it easy to outwit Zeus, who was busy with many things.

Once she persuaded the other gods into a plot

against him. She drugged his drink; they surrounded him as he slept and bound him with rawhide thongs. He raged and roared and swore to destroy them, but they had stolen his thunderbolt, and he could not break the thongs.

But his faithful cousin, the Hundred-handed Briareus, who had helped him against the Titans, was working as his gardener. He heard the quarreling under the palace window, looked in, and saw his master bound to the couch. He reached through with his hundred long arms and unbound the hundred knots.

Zeus jumped from the couch and seized his thunderbolt. The terrified plotters fell to their knees, weeping and pleading. He seized Hera and hung her in the sky, binding her with golden chains. And the others did not dare to rescue her, although her voice was like the wind sobbing. But her weeping kept Zeus awake. In the morning he said he would free her if she swore never to rebel again. She promised, and Zeus promised to mend his ways too. But they kept watching each other.

Zeus was king of the gods, lord of the sky. His sister Demeter was the earth-goddess, lady of growing things. His sister Hera, queen of the gods, was also his wife. His brother Poseidon was god of the sea. His other brother, Hades, ruled a dark domain, the underworld, the land beyond death.

The other gods in the Pantheon were Zeus's children; three of them were also Hera's. These were Ares, the god of war; Hephaestus, the smith-god, forger of weapons; and Eris, goddess of discord, who shrieks beside Ares in his battle chariot. The rest of Zeus's children were born out of wedlock. Three of them entered the Pantheon.

The first was Athene, and the story of how she was born is told in the next chapter.

Athene

Zeus was strolling on Olympus one morning and noticed a new maiden walking in his garden. She was Metis, a Titaness, daughter of one of his old enemies. But the war was long ago, and she was beautiful. He charged down the slope after her.

She turned into a hawk and flew away. He turned into a hawk and flew after her. She flew over the lake and dived in and became a fish. He became a fish and swam after her. She climbed on the bank and became a serpent and wriggled away. He changed himself into a serpent and wriggled after her and caught her. And the two serpents plaited themselves into beautiful loops.

After he left her, he heard a bird cry and a fish leap, and those wild sounds combined to become a prophecy, which the rattling leaves echoed: "Oh, Zeus, Metis will bear a child, a girl child. But if she bears again, it will be a son who will depose you as you deposed Cronos."

The next day Zeus walked in his garden again and found Metis there. This time she did not flee. He spoke softly to her and smiled. She came to him. Suddenly he opened his mouth and swallowed her.

That afternoon he suffered a headache—the worst headache that anyone, god or mortal, had suffered since the beginning of time. It was exactly as if someone were inside him with a spear, thrusting at all the soft places in his head. He shouted for Hephaestus, who came rushing up with hammer and wedge. Zeus put his head on the anvil, and Hephaestus split the mighty skull. Then Hephaestus leaped back, frightened, because out of the head sprang a tall maiden in armor, holding a long spear.

This was Athene, the gray-eyed, the wide-browed. The manner of her birth gave her domain over intellectual activities. It was she who taught man how to use tools. She taught him to invent the ax, the plough, the ox-yoke, the wheel, and the sail. She taught his wife to spin and weave. She concocted the science of numbers and taught it to man—but never to woman. She hated Ares and took great pleasure in thwarting him on the field of battle. For all his mighty strength, she often beat him, because she was a mistress of strategy. Before battle, captains prayed to her for tactics. Before trial, judges prayed to her for wisdom. It was she who stated that compassion was the best part of wisdom. The other gods didn't know what she meant by this. But some men understood and were grateful. All in all, she was perhaps the best-loved god in the Pantheon. The people of Athens named their beautiful city after her.

There are many stories about Athene—about her skill in battle, her wisdom, and her kindliness. But, like the other gods, she was also very jealous. One of the best stories is that of Arachne.

Arachne was a young girl who lived in Lydia, famous for its purple dye. Her joy was weaving, and she wove the most beautiful things anyone had ever seen: cloaks so light you could not feel them about your shoulders, but warmer than fur; tapestries wrought with pictures so marvelous that birds would fly through the window and try to eat the cherries off the woven bough. She was a very young girl, and everyone praised her—and soon she began to praise herself. She said:

"I, I am the greatest weaver in all the world. The greatest since the world began, no doubt. In fact, I can weave better than Athene herself."

Athene heard this, of course. The gods are very quick to hear criticism and very swift to act. So she came to earth, to the little village where Arachne lived.

The girl was inside, spinning. She heard a knock at the door and opened it. There stood a lady so tall, so sternly beautiful that Arachne knew she must be a goddess, and she was afraid she knew which one. She fell on her knees. Far above her head she heard a voice speaking softly, saying terrible things.

"Yes, miserable girl, I am Athene. I am the goddess you have mocked. Is there any reason I should not kill you?"

Arachne shook her head, weeping. She could not answer.

"Very well," said Athene. "Prepare yourself for death. You have defied the gods and must die."

Then Arachne stood up and said, "Before I die, great Athene, let me give you a present." She went in and took a lovely cloak she had woven and gave it to her. And said: "Take this cloak. It must often get cold up high on Olympus. This will shield you from the wind. Please take it. I am sure you have nothing so fine."

Athene shook her head and said, "Poor child. You are being destroyed by your own worth. Your talent has poisoned you with pride like the sting of a scorpion. So that which makes beauty brings death. But it is a handsome cloak, and I appreciate the gift. I will give you one chance. You have boasted that you can spin and weave better than I—than I, who invented the loom, the distaff and the spindle, and out of the fleece of the clouds wove the first counterpane for my father, Zeus, who likes to sleep warm, and dyed it with the colors of the sunset. But you say you can weave better than I. Very well, you shall have a chance to prove it. And your own villagers shall judge. Seven days from today, we shall meet. You will set your spindle in that meadow, and I shall be in my place, and we shall have a contest. You will weave what you will, and I shall do so too. Then we will show what we have done, and the people will judge. If you win, I shall withdraw the punishment. If you lose, it is your life. Do you agree?"

"Oh, yes," said Arachne. "Thank you, dear goddess, for sparing my life."

"It is not yet spared," said Athene.

The word flashed from village to village. When the time came, not only Arachne's neighbors but all the people in the land had gathered in the great meadow to watch the contest. Arachne's house was the last in the village and faced the great meadow. She had set up her loom outside the door. Athene sat on a low flat hill overlooking the field. Her loom was as large as Arachne's cottage.

The girl went first. At the sight of her sitting spinning there in the sunlight, the crowd pushed in so close she hardly had room to work. Her white hands danced among the flax, and she worked so quickly, so deftly, that she seemed to have forgotten the loom and to be weaving in the air. Swiftly and more swiftly she tapped on the wool with her fingers, making it billow and curl, then rolling it quickly into a ball, then shaking it out again, straining the wool into long shining threads with quick little pokes of her thumb at her spindle. It was said that her working was as beautiful as her work, and when she was told that, she always smiled and said, "It is the same thing." So she wove, and the people watched. Then the finished cloth began to come from the loom, and everybody laughed to see. For they were joyous scenes. Morning scenes: a little boy and a little girl running in a green field among yellow flowers, chased by a black dog; a maiden at a window dreamily combing her hair; a young man watching the sea, counting the waves. And, later, in a purple dusk, that same young man and girl standing under a tree looking at each other. Swiftly and more swiftly the white hands danced between loom and spindle. She wove bouquets of flowers for the wedding, and a wedding gown for the bride, and a gorgeous cloak for the young husband. And, remembering what Athene had said before, she spun a counterpane for their bed. Each square not a block of color, but a little picture—one from the childhood of the man, one from the childhood of the bride, all together, mixing, as their memories would mix now.

The counterpane was last. When she arose and snapped it out, the people gasped and laughed and wept with joy. And Arachne curtsied toward the low hill, and Athene began to spin.

The goddess had conjured up a flock of plump white woolly clouds about her hilltop. So she did not have to comb fleece or draw thread; she used cloudwool, the finest stuff in all the world. And she dyed it with the colors of the dawn and the colors of the sunset and the colors of sleep and the colors of storm. Now the whole western part of the sky was her loom. She flung great tapestries across the horizon. Scenes from Olympus—things that mortal man had never hoped to see. Almost too terrible to see . . . Cronos cutting up Oranos with a scythe . . . Zeus charging across the firmament with his Hundred-handed Ones, shattering the Titans . . . the binding of Zeus . . . the punishment of Hera. Zeus chasing Metis as hawk and fish and snake. Then the birth of Athene herself, springing from Zeus' broken head. Then more quiet scenes: Athene teaching the arts to man; teaching him to plough, to sail, to ride in chariots; teaching the women to spin. Then, finally— muddling it all up, poking her long spindle among the woven clouds, and mixing them and stirring up a dark strange picture—the future of man. Man growing huge and monstrous, his trees turning to spikes, his fields to stone. Swollen and dropsical with pride, building something so loathsome he had to look away while he was making it.

This was too much for the multitude. The vast crowd fell on its knees and wept. Arachne was watching. She had never moved from the time Athene had started to work, but stood there straight with pale face and glittering eyes, watching. And when the people fell on their knees, she turned and went away. She walked quietly to a grove of trees and there took a rope and hanged herself.

Athene came down from the hill and spoke no word to the people, who dispersed. Then she went to the grove and saw Arachne hanging there. The girl's face was black, her eyes were bulging, her hair was streaming. Athene reached her long arm and touched the girl on the shoulder. The face grew blacker, and the eyes bulged more. The body shrank; the arms and legs dwindled and multiplied. Then Athene touched the rope. It shriveled, growing thinner and thinner, until it was a frail shining strand. And there at the end of this shining silken hair swung a small hairy creature with many legs.

It looked at Athene, then turned and scuttled up its thread, drawing it up as it climbed. It floated away over the grass until it came to a low bush, cast another loop, and sat there practicing, for it knew that now it was meant to spin without rivalry until the end of time.

That is why spiders are called Arachnids by those who know them best.

Poseidon

After Cronos was deposed, the three sons threw dice for his empire. Zeus, the youngest, won and chose the sky. Poseidon smiled to himself because the sky was empty, and he knew that the impulsive Zeus had chosen it because it looked so high. And now, he, Poseidon, could choose as he would have done if he had won. He chose the sea. He had always wanted it; it is the best place for adventures and secrets and makes claim on land and

15

sky. Hades, who was always unlucky, had to take the underworld. The earth was held as a commonwealth and left to the goddesses to manage.

Poseidon left Olympus and came to his kingdom. He immediately set about building a huge underwater palace with a great pearl and coral throne. He needed a queen and chose Thetis, a beautiful Nereid, or water nymph. But it was prophesied that any son born to Thetis would be greater than his father, so Poseidon decided to try elsewhere. The prophecy came true. The son of Thetis was Achilles.

Poseidon chose another Nereid named Amphitrite. But like his brother Zeus, he was a great traveler and had hundreds of children in different places. He was a very difficult god, changeful and quarrelsome. He did bear grudges; but he could be pleased, and then his smile was radiant. He liked jokes and thought up very curious forms for his creatures. He liked to startle nymphs with monsters, and concocted the octopus, the squid, the sea-polyp or jellyfish, the swordfish, blowfish, sea cow, and many others. Once, trying to appease Amphitrite's jealous rage, he thought up the dolphin and gave it to her as a gift.

He was greedy and aggressive, always trying to add to his kingdom. Once he claimed Attica as his own and stabbed his trident into the hillside where the Acropolis still stands, and a spring of salt water spouted. Now, the people of Athens did not want to belong to the kingdom of the sea. They were afraid of Poseidon, who had a habit of seizing all the youth of a town when he was in the mood. So they prayed to be put under the protection of another god. Athene heard their prayers. She came down and planted an olive tree by the side of the spring. Poseidon was enraged. His face darkened, and he roared with fury, raising a storm. A fishing fleet was blown off the sea and never came to port. He challenged Athene to single combat and threatened to stir up a tidal wave to break over the city if she refused. She accepted. But Zeus heard the sound of this quarreling and came down and decreed a truce. Then all the gods sat in council to hear the rival claims. After hearing both Athene and Poseidon, they voted to award the city to Athene because her olive tree was the better gift. After that, Athenians had to be very careful when they went to sea, and were often unfortunate in their naval battles.

Poseidon was very fond of Demeter and pursued her hotly whenever he thought about it. He cornered her finally one hot afternoon in a mountain pass, and demanded that she love him. She didn't know what to do—he was so huge, so implacable, so persistent.

Finally Demeter said, "Give me a gift. You have made creatures for the sea; now make me a land animal. But a beautiful one, the most beautiful ever seen."

She thought she was safe, because she believed he could make only monsters. She was amazed when he made her a horse, and gasped with delight when she saw it. And Poseidon was so struck by his handiwork that he swiftly made a herd of horses that began to gallop about the meadow, tossing their heads, flirting their tails, kicking up their back legs, and neighing joyously. And he was so fascinated by the horses that he forgot all about Demeter and leaped on one and rode off. Later he made another herd of green ones for his undersea stables. But Demeter kept the first herd; from that all the horses in the world have descended.

Another story says it took Poseidon a full week to make the horse. During that time he made and cast aside many other creatures that didn't come out right. But he simply threw them away without killing them, and they made their way into the world. From them have come the camel, the hippopotamus, the giraffe, the donkey, and the zebra.

In another story, Demeter turned herself into a mare to escape Poseidon. But he immediately changed himself into a stallion, galloped after her, and caught her. From this courtship came a wild horse, Arion, and the nymph named Despoena.

Demeter was also a moon goddess. And all through mythology there is a connection between horse and moon and sea. The she-horse is given a sea-name, "mare"; the moon swings the tides, the waves have white manes, the dripping horses stamp on the beach, and their hooves leave moon-shaped marks. An old, old thing that has not entirely disappeared.

Hades

When the Greeks buried their dead, they put a coin under the corpse's tongue so that his soul could pay the fare on the ferry that crossed the river Styx. It was Charon who rowed the boat; he was a miser. Souls who couldn't pay for the ride had to wait on this side of the river. Sometimes they came back to haunt those who hadn't given them the fare.

On the other side of the river was a great wall. Its

gate was guarded by Cerberus, a three-headed dog who
had an appetite for live meat and attacked everyone but
spirits. Beyond the gate, in Tartarus, was a great wide
field shaded by black poplars. Here lived the dead—
heroes and cowards, soldiers, shepherds, priests, minstrels, slaves. They wandered back and forth aimlessly.
When they spoke, they twittered like bats. Here they
awaited trial by three judges—Minos, Rhadamanthys,
and Aeacus.

Those who had particularly displeased the gods
were given special punishment. Sisyphus must always
push a huge rock uphill. Each time he gets it halfway
up, it breaks loose and rolls down to the bottom, and
he must begin again. And this he will do for all time.
Tantalus has been given a burning thirst and set chin-
deep in a cool, clear stream of water. But every time he
bends to put his lips to the water, it shrinks away, and he
can never drink. Here he will stand as long as Sisyphus
rolls his stone.

But these are special cases. Most of the souls were
judged to be not too good and not too bad, but simply
dead. They went back to the field, which is called the
Field of Asphodel, to wait—for nothing.

Those judged to be of unusual virtue went to the
Elysian Fields close by. Here it was always holiday.
The air was full of music. The shades danced and
played all day long—all night long too—for the dead
need no sleep. Also, these happy spirits had the option
of being reborn on earth. Only the bravest accepted.
There was a special part of Elysium called the Isles of
the Blest. Here lived those who had been three times
born and three times gained Elysium.

Hades and his queen lived in a great palace made of
black rock. He was very jealous of his brothers and
scarcely ever left his domain. He was fiercely posses-
sive, gloated over every new arrival, and demanded a

headcount from Charon at the close of each day. Never did he allow any of his subjects to escape. Nor did he allow a mortal to visit Tartarus and return. There were only two exceptions to this rule, and those are other stories.

The palace grounds and the surrounding fields were called Erebus; this was the deepest part of the underworld. No birds flew here, but the sound of wings was heard; for here lived the Erinyes, or Furies, who were older than the gods. Their names were Tisiphone, Alecto, and Megaera. They were hags, with snaky hair, red-hot eyes, and yellow teeth. They slashed the air with metal-studded whips, and when they found a victim, they whipped the flesh from his bones. Their task was to visit earth and punish evil-doers, especially those who had escaped other punishment. They were greatly feared; no one dared say their name. But they were referred to as the "Eumenides," or Kindly Ones. Hades valued them. They enriched his kingdom, for their attentions persuaded people to suicide. He enjoyed their conversation. When they returned to Erebus after their work was done, they circled low over the palace grounds, screaming their tale, and the latest gossip.

Hades was well-cast to rule the dead. He was violent, loathed change, and was given to slow black rage. His most dramatic hour was when he kidnaped Persephone and made her his queen. But that belongs to the next story.

Demeter

Demeter means "Barley-mother." Another name for her is Ceres, from which we get the word "cereal." She was the goddess of the cornfield, mistress of planting and harvesting, lady of growing things. Zeus was very fond of her. He always obliged her with rain when her fields were thirsty. He gave her two children, a boy and a girl. The girl was named Persephone, and Demeter loved her very much.

Persephone was raised among flowers and looked like a flower herself. Her body was as pliant as a stem, her skin soft as petals, and she had pansy eyes. She took charge of flowers for her mother. She was adept at making up new kinds and naming them.

One day she went farther than usual—across a stream, through a grove of trees, to a little glade. She carried her paintpot, for she had seen a stand of tall waxy lilies she had decided to stripe. As she was painting their faces she saw a bush she hadn't noticed before. She went to look at it. It was a very strange bush, with thick, green, glossy leaves and hung with large red berries that trembled on their stems like drops of blood. She stared at the bush. She didn't know whether she liked it or not. She decided she did not and seized it by its branches and pulled. But it was toughly rooted and hard to pull. She was used to getting her own way. She set herself and gave a mighty tug. Up came the bush; its long roots dragged out of the ground, leaving a big hole. She tossed the bush aside and turned to go back to her lilies, but she heard a rumbling sound and turned back. The noise that grew louder and louder was coming from the hole. To her horror, the hole seemed to be spreading, opening like a mouth, and the rumbling grew to a jangling, crashing din.

Out of the hole leaped six black horses, dragging behind them a golden chariot. In the chariot stood a tall figure in a flowing black cape. On his head was a black crown. She had no time to scream. He reached out his long arm, snatched her into the chariot, and lashed his horses. They curvetted in the air and plunged into the hole again. When they had gone, the hole closed.

Demeter was frantic when the girl didn't come home, and rushed out to search for her. The tall green-clad goddess rode in a light wicker chariot behind a swift white horse, a gift from Poseidon. She sped here

and there, calling, "Persephone . . . Persephone . . ."
But no one answered. All night long she searched, and
as dawn broke, she came to the glade. There she saw
the uprooted bush and the trampled grass. She leaped
from her chariot. Then she saw something that stabbed
her through—Persephone's little paintpot, overturned.
She lifted her head to the sky and howled like a she-
wolf. Then she fell still and listened. The sun was rising; the birds had begun to gossip. They told each other
of the heedless girl and the strange bush and the hole
and the chariot and the black rider and how surprised
the girl was when he caught her.

Then Demeter spoke softly, questioning the birds.
They told her enough for her to know who had taken
her daughter. She put her face in her hands and wept.
Just then a little boy came running into the meadow to
pick some flowers. When he saw Demeter, he laughed.
He had never seen a grownup crying before. But when
she looked up, he stopped laughing. She pointed at him,
whispering, and he was immediately changed into a
lizard. But he hadn't learned to scuttle yet and just sat
there looking at Demeter a moment too long, for a
hawk swooped and caught him. He was a lizard for
only a short while.

Demeter climbed back into her chariot and sped to
Olympus. She charged into the throne room where Zeus
sat.

"Justice!" she cried. "Justice! Your brother Hades
has stolen my daughter—*our* daughter."

"Peace, good sister," said Zeus. "Compose yourself.
Hades' wooing has been a trifle abrupt, perhaps, but after all he is my brother—*our* brother—and is accounted
a good match. Think, sweet Demeter. It is difficult for
our daughter to look beyond the family without marry-
ing far beneath her."

"Never!" cried Demeter. "It must not be! Anyone

but Hades! Don't you realize this is a spring child, a flower child, a delicate unopened bud. No ray of sunlight ever pierces that dank hole he calls his kingdom. She'll wither and die."

"She is our daughter," said Zeus. "I fancy she has a talent for survival. Pray, think it over."

Then Demeter noticed that Zeus was holding a new thunderbolt, a marvelously wrought zigzag lance of lightning, volt-blue, radiant with energy. And she realized that Hades, who in his deep realms held all stores of silver and gold, had sent Zeus a special gift. It would be difficult to obtain justice.

"Once again," she said, "will you restore my daughter to me?"

"My dear," said Zeus, "when your rage cools, you will realize that this is a fine match, the very best thing for the child. Please, go back to earth and give yourself a chance to be intelligent about this."

"I will go back to earth," said Demeter, "and I will not return until you send for me."

Weeks passed. Then Zeus found his sleep being disturbed by sounds of lamentation. He looked down upon the earth and saw a grievous sight. Nothing grew. The fields were blasted and parched. Trees were stripped of leaves, standing blighted, with the blazing sun beating down. The soil was hard and cracked, covered with the shriveled brown husks of wheat and corn and barley killed in the bud. And there was no green place anywhere. The people were starving; the cattle had nothing to eat; the game could find nothing and had fled. And a great wailing and lamentation arose as the people lifted their faces to Olympus and prayed for Zeus to help them.

"Well," he thought to himself, fingering his new thunderbolt, "I suppose we shall have to compromise."

He sent for Demeter. When she came, he said, "I

have been thinking. Perhaps I have not been quite fair to you."

"No," said Demeter.

"Do you still wish your daughter's return?"

"Yes," said Demeter. "While she is gone, no crops will grow. No tree will bear, no grass will spring. While she is gone and while I mourn, the earth will grow as dry and shriveled as my heart and will put forth no green thing."

"Very well," said Zeus. "In light of all the facts, this is my judgment. Your daughter shall be restored to you and shall remain with you. However, if any food has passed her lips during her sojourn in Tartarus, then she must remain there. This is the Law of Abode, older than our decrees, and even I am powerless to revoke it."

"She will have been too sad to eat," cried Demeter. "No food will have passed her lips. She shall return to me and remain with me. You have spoken, and I hold you to your word."

Zeus whistled, and Hermes, the messenger god, appeared. Zeus sent him with a message to Hades demanding Persephone's release.

"Will you ride with me to the gates of Tartarus?" cried Demeter. "I have the swiftest horse in the world, given me by Poseidon."

"Thank you, good aunt," said Hermes. "But I believe my winged shoes are even faster."

And he flew out of the window.

In the meantime, Persephone was in Erebus with the dark king. After the first few days of haste and brutality and strangeness, he began to treat her very gently, and with great kindness. He gave her rubies and diamonds to play jacks with, had dresses spun for her of gold and silver thread, ordered her a throne of the finest ebony, and gave her a crown of black pearls. But she made herself very difficult to please. She tossed her head, stamped her foot, and turned from him. She would not speak to him and said she would never forgive him. She said she wanted to go home to her mother, and that she had to attend to her flowers, and that she hated him and always would. As she launched these tirades at him, he would stand and listen and frown and keep listening until she flounced away. Then he would go and get her another gift.

Secretly, though, so secretly that she didn't even tell it to herself, she was rather enjoying the change. She did miss the sunshine and the flowers, but there was much to amuse her. Secretly she gloated upon her power over this most fearsome monarch. Secretly she enjoyed his gifts and his efforts to please her . . . and marveled at the way he was obeyed. Although she never forgot how he had frightened her when he came charging out of that hole in his chariot, she admired the lofty set of his black-robed figure, the majestic shoulders, the great impatient hands, and his gloomy black eyes. But she knew that part of her power over him was disdain, and so kept flouting and abusing him, and, which made him gloomier than ever, refused to let a crumb of food pass her lips.

He tried every way he knew to tempt her into eating. His cook prepared the most delicious meals, and his servants bore them to her chamber. But she would pretend not to notice a thing and sit there holding her head high, not even allowing her nostrils to twitch, although the rich smells were making her wild with hunger. She swore she would not eat a mouthful until he had returned her to her mother.

He was desperate to please her. He set aside a corner of the palace grounds for a dark garden and gave her rare seeds to plant—magical blooms that did not need the sunlight. She grew a species of black orchid and mushrooms and nightshade, henbane, and hellebore. He

gave her a little boy to help her garden, a very clever little gardener, a new spirit. He was very deft and good
company too, although she noticed that his eyes were a
bit lidless. She had no way of knowing that he was the
same little boy her mother had turned into a lizard and
fed to a hawk. But he knew who she was.

She had other amusements too. She liked to wander
in the Elysian Fields and dance with the happy shades.
She was fascinated by the torments, particularly the
funny man trying to roll the stone uphill and always
having to start over again. She pitied Tantalus, and
when no one was looking, cupped some water in her
hands and gave it to him to drink. And he thanked her in
a deep sad voice. But after she left, it was worse than
ever; he knew she would not remember him again, and
this one flash of hope made the ordeal worse.

Still, she liked her garden best, and that was where
she spent most of her time—more time than ever, because she was so hungry she didn't know what to do,
and she didn't want Hades to see how she felt. She
knew he would think up more delicious things to tempt
her if he thought she was weakening.

Standing in the garden one afternoon, half-hidden in
a clump of nightshade, she saw the little boy eating
something. It was a red fruit, and he was eating it
juicily. He saw her watching and came toward her smiling, his mouth stained with red juice. He held out his
hand. It was a pomegranate, her favorite fruit.

"We're alone," he whispered. "No one will see you.
No one will know. Quickly now—eat!"

She looked about. It was true. No one could see
them. She felt her hands acting by themselves, as
though she had nothing to do with them. She watched
as the fingers curled savagely and ripped the fruit
across. They dug in, plucked out seeds, and offered
them to her lips. One . . . two . . . three . . . she thought
she had never tasted anything so delicious as these tiny

tart juicy seeds. Just as she swallowed her sixth seed, a high glad yelling cry split the air, and the pomegranate dropped to the ground. It was a cry that any god recognized—Hermes' keen herald shout, meaning that he was coming with news, good or bad, but worthy of high attention.

She raced to the palace. The little gardener scooped up the pomegranate and raced after her. Sure enough, it was cousin Hermes, his hair tumbled from the wind, the wings on his feet still fluttering from the speed of his going.

"Good day, cousin," he said.

Hades loomed next to him, scowling blackly.

"I bring you a message from your mother. She wants you home. And your host has kindly agreed to an early departure. How are you? Haven't eaten anything here, I hope. No? Good! Let's be on our way."

He put his arm around her waist, and they rose in the air. And Persephone, looking back, saw the little gardener rush to Hades with the pomegranate in his hand.

By the time Persephone had come home to her mother, Hades had already been to Olympus and had presented his case to Zeus. Zeus pronounced his judgment. Because the girl had eaten six seeds of the pomegranate, she would have to spend six months with Hades each year.

"Never mind, Mother," said Persephone. "Don't cry. We must be happy for the time that I am here."

"I suffer!" cried Demeter. "I suffer! Here—" She struck herself on the chest. "Here—in my mother's heart. And if I suffer then everyone else shall suffer too. For the months that you spend with that scoundrel, no grass will grow, no flowers blow, no trees will bear. So long as you are below, there will be desolation everywhere."

That is why summer and winter are the way they are. That is why there is a time for planting and a time when the earth must sleep under frost.

Birth of the Twins

Zeus pursued a nymph named Leto. But Hera was watching, so he changed Leto into a quail, and then himself into a quail, and they met in a glade. Here the sun sifted through the trees and striped the grass with shadows, and it was difficult to see two quail whose feathers were brown and lighter brown. But the eyes of jealousy are very sharp, and Hera saw them. She flung a curse, saying, "Leto, you will grow heavy with child, but you shall not bear anywhere the sun shines."

She sent the great serpent Python to enforce her curse, to hunt Leto out of any sunny place she might try to rest. Zeus sent the south wind to help the girl, and she was carried on the wings of the warm strong wind to an island called Delos. Python swam after. Before he could reach the island, however, Zeus unmoored it and sent it floating swiftly away, pushed by the south wind, more swiftly than Python could swim. Here, on this lovely island, Leto gave birth to twins—Artemis and Apollo.

Artemis

Father Zeus was by no means an attentive parent. He had so many children in so many different circumstances he could scarcely keep them all in mind. However, he was not permitted to forget Leto's children. They were too beautiful. And beauty was the quality he found most attractive. As he looked down from Olympus, their faces seemed to blaze from among all the children on earth. It seemed to him that they cast their own light, these twins, each one different—Apollo a ruddy light, Artemis a silver light. And he knew that they were true godlings and must be brought to Olympus.

He sent for them on their third birthday. He had Hephaestus make Apollo a golden bow and a quiver of golden arrows that could never be emptied and a golden chariot drawn by golden ponies. But he withheld Artemis' gifts; he preferred her and he wanted her to ask him for things. He took her on his lap and said, "And what gifts would you fancy, little maid?"

She said, "I wish to be your maiden always, never a woman. And I want many names in case I get bored with one. I want a bow and arrow too—but silver, not gold. I want an embroidered deerskin tunic short enough to run in. I need fifty ocean nymphs to sing for me, and twenty wood nymphs to hunt with me. And I want a pack of hounds, please—fierce, swift ones. I want the mountains for my special places, and one city. One will be enough; I don't like cities." She reached up and played with his beard and smiled at him. "Yes? May I have all these things? May I?"

Zeus answered, "For a child like you, it is worthwhile braving Hera's wrath once in a while. You shall have more than you ask for. You shall have the gift of eternal chastity, and also the gift of changing your mind about it at any time, which will help you not to want to. And, finally, the greatest gift of all: You shall go out and choose your own gifts so that they will have a special value."

She kissed him and whispered her thanks into his ear and then went running off to choose her gifts. She went to the woods and to the river and to the ocean stream and selected the most beautiful nymphs for her court. She visited Hephaestus in his smoking smithy inside the mountain and said, "I've come for my bow. A silver one, please."

He said, "Silver is more difficult to work than gold. It needs cool light; it should be made underwater. You must go deep beneath the sea, off the island of Lipara, where my Cyclopes are making a horse trough for Poseidon, who thinks of nothing but horses these days."

So Artemis and her nymphs swam underwater to where the Cyclopes were hammering at a great trough. The nymphs were frightened at the sight of the huge one-eyed scowling brutes, and they hated the noise of the hammering. But Artemis jumped up on the forge and said, "I come with a message from Hephaestus. He bids you put aside this horse trough and make me a silver bow and a quiver of silver arrows which will fill again as soon as it is empty. If you do this, I shall give you the first game I shoot." The Cyclopes, who were very greedy and tired of working on the horse trough, agreed.

When they had finished her bow, she thanked them very prettily. But when their leader, Brontes, tried to take her on his knee, she tore a great handful of hair from his chest. He put her down quickly and went away cursing.

Holding her silver bow high, screaming with joy, she raced across field and valley and hill, followed by her nymphs who streamed after her with flashing knees and floating hair laughing and singing. She came to Arcadia where Pan was feeding his hounds.

"Oh, Pan," she cried. "Oh, little king of the wood, my favorite cousin, please give me some of your dogs—the best ones, please."

"And what will you give me in return?" he said, looking at the nymphs.

"Choose," she said, "But I should warn you, cousin, that like me they have taken an unbreakable vow of chastity."

"Never mind," said Pan. "Keep them. What dogs do you fancy?"

"That one and that one and that one," she cried, "and this one. And I must have him . . . and him."

He gave her his ten best dogs. Three of them were huge black and white hounds able to catch a live lion and drag it back to the hunter. The others were lean white deerhounds; any one of them could outrun a stag.

Artemis was wild to try out her new gifts. She sent her white hounds racing after two deer, bidding them bring back the animals unharmed. She harnessed the deer to her silver chariot and drove away. She saw a tree which had been struck by lightning; it was still smoldering. She had her nymphs break pine branches and thrust them into the cinders, for night was coming and she wanted light to shoot by. She was too impatient to wait for dawn.

Four times she shot her silver bow. First she split a pine tree, then an olive tree. Then she shot a wild boar. Lastly, she shot an arrow into a city of unjust men, and the arrow pierced all of them, never ceasing its flight till they were all dead.

And the people, seeing her ride over the mountains,

wielding her silver bow, followed by the maidens and their torches, called her the Goddess of the Moon. Some called her the Maiden of the Silver Bow. Others called her Lady of the Wild Things. Some called her the Huntress. Others, simply, the Maiden. And so she had her last gift—many names.

She let no man approach her. Once a young man named Actaeon glimpsed her bathing in a stream. She was so beautiful he could not bear to go away, but hid there, watching. She saw him and immediately changed him into a stag. Then she whistled up her hounds, who tore him to pieces.

She tried to impose the same rule upon her nymphs, which was difficult. Zeus himself seduced one of the most beautiful, named Callisto. When Artemis learned of this, she changed Callisto into a she-bear and whistled to her dogs. They came leaping and howling and would have torn the bear to pieces too, but Zeus happened to notice what was going on. He caught Callisto up and set her among the stars, still in her bear shape so that Hera would not be suspicious.

Once Artemis found her vow difficult to keep. But that is another story, the story of Orion, which comes later.

Apollo

Apollo was the most beautiful of the gods. His hair was dark gold, his eyes stormy blue. He wore a tunic of golden panther skin, carried his golden bow, and wore a quiver of golden arrows. His chariot was beaten gold; its horses were white with golden manes and flame-colored eyes. He was god of the sun always. Later he became patron of music, poetry, mathematics, and medicine. And, later, when he was a mature god, he preached moderation. He bade his worshippers to look first into their own hearts and find there the beginnings of wisdom and to conduct themselves prudently in all things. But in his youth he did many cruel and wanton deeds. Several times he was almost expelled from the company of the gods by Zeus whom he had angered with his wild folly.

As soon as he was given his bow and arrows, he raced down from Olympus to hunt the Python who had hunted his mother. Dryads, who are tattletales, told him he could find his enemy at Mount Parnassus. There he sped. As he stood on a hill, he saw the great serpent weaving its dusty coils far below. He notched an arrow, drew his bow, and let fly. It darted like light; he saw it strike, saw the huge coils flail in agony. Shouting with savage glee, he raced down the slope, but when he got there he found the serpent gone. It had left a trail of blood which he followed to the oracle of Mother Earth at Delphi. Python was hiding in a cave, where he could not be followed. Apollo breathed on his arrowheads and shot them into the cave as fast as he could. They broke into flames when they hit. Smoke filled the cave, and the serpent had to crawl out. Apollo, standing on a rock, shot him so full of arrows he looked like a porcupine. He skinned the great snake and saved the hide for a gift.

Now, it was a sacred place where he had done his killing; here lived the oracles of Mother Earth, whom the gods themselves consulted. They were priestesses, trained from infancy. They chewed laurel, built fire of magic herbs, and sat in the smoke, which threw them into a trance wherein they saw—and told in riddles—what was to come. Knowing that he had already violated a shrine, Apollo thought he might as well make his deed as large as possible, and claimed the oracles for his own—bidding them to prophesy in his name.

When Mother Earth complained to Zeus about the killing of her Python, Apollo smoothly promised to make amends. He instituted annual games at Delphi in celebration of his victory, and these he graciously named after his enemy, calling them the Pythian games. And he named the oracles Pythonesses.

Less excusable was Apollo's treatment of a satyr named Marsyas. This happy fellow had the misfortune to be an excellent musician—a realm Apollo considered his own—and where he would brook no rivalry. Hearing the satyr praised too often, Apollo invited him to a contest. The winner was to choose a penalty to which the loser would have to submit, and the Muses were to judge. So Marsyas played his flute, and Apollo played his lyre. They played exquisitely; the Muses could not choose between them. Then Apollo shouted, "Now you must turn your instrument upside down, and play and sing at the same time. That is the rule. I go first." Thereupon the god turned his lyre upside down, and played and sang a hymn praising the gods, and especially their beautiful daughters, the Muses. But you cannot play a flute upside down, and certainly cannot sing while playing it, so Marsyas was declared the loser. Apollo collected his price. He flayed Marsyas alive and nailed his skin to a tree. A stream gushed from the tree's roots and became a river. On the banks of that river grew reeds which sang softly when the wind blew. People called the river Marsyas, and that is still its name.

Sons of Apollo

During the contest with the satyr Marsyas, Apollo won the favor of the most playful Muse, Thalia, queen of festivities. Upon her he fathered the Corybantes, or crested dancers, lithe young men who shaved their hair to a forelock and danced at great rituals.

Then, roaming the hillsides, he came across a young girl who reminded him of his sister. She was a huntress. She chased deer on foot, hunted bears and wolves. When he saw her wrestling a full-grown lion and throwing it to earth, he decided he must have her. Her name was Cyrene. The son he gave her was named Aristeus, who taught man beekeeping, olive culture, cheese-making, and many other useful arts.

His next adventure was with the nymph Dryope. He found her tending sheep on a mountainside. He hid behind a tree and watched her. To his dismay, she was joined by a gaggle of hamadryads, mischievous girls who love to tell tales. So he had to stay hidden. He waited for the hamadryads to leave, but they lingered. Gods are impatient; they hate to be kept waiting. He changed himself into a tortoise and crawled out. The nymphs were delighted to see him and turned him this way and that and tickled him with a straw. He was a splendid glossy tortoise with a beautiful black and green shell. Dryope wanted him for her own and put him in her tunic. When her friends protested, he turned himself into a snake, poked his head out of the tunic, and hissed at them. The hamadryads fled, screaming. Dryope fainted. When she came to, she was in the arms of a god. Their son was Amphissus, founder of cities and builder of temples.

But his most famous son was Asclepius. This was the manner of his birth.

Apollo fell in love with Coronis, a princess of Thessaly, and insisted on having his way, which was unwise of him because she loved an Arcadian prince named Ischys. When she was with child, Apollo went on a journey, but set a white crow to spy on her. All crows were white then and were excellent chaperons; they had sharp eyes and jeering voices.

It was to Delphi that Apollo had gone. An oracle there told him that at that very moment Coronis was entertaining young Ischys. Just then the crow flew in, wildly excited, full of scandal, telling the same tale. "Your fault! You did not watch her closely enough!" cried Apollo. And he cursed the crow with a curse so furious that her feathers were scorched—and all crows have been black ever since.

Apollo could not bring himself to kill Coronis. So he asked his sister Artemis to oblige him. She was happy to; she was never fond of his amours. She sped to Thessaly and finished Coronis with one arrow.

Apollo, very dejected, put the corpse on the funeral pyre and lighted the fire. Then he remembered that she was with child by him. Hermes was now standing by, waiting to conduct her soul to Tartarus, for that was one of his duties. Understanding the situation in a flash, he delivered the dead girl of a living child, a boy. Apollo wished to have nothing to do with the child and asked Hermes to take care of him. Hermes had been struck by the way the baby had observed the details of his own birth—watching everything with a wide stare, so interested he forgot to cry—and recognized that this was an unusual child. So he gave him into the care of Chiron, the centaur, the fabulous tutor. Chiron taught him diagnostics, surgery, herbology, and hunting.

The boy could not wait to grow up. He doctored

everyone he could get his hands on, and was soon known throughout the land for his skill at curing the sick. His fame reached Apollo, who decided to test him. He appeared at Asclepius' door in the guise of a feeble old man afflicted with every loathsome disease known to medicine—and a pauper besides. Asclepius tended him with his own hands, and was so gentle and skillful that Apollo was amazed. The god resumed his own form and embraced the lad and told him he was pleased with his progress. He sent him to see his aunt Athene, who, he said, knew certain secrets of mortality. She too approved of the young man and gave him two vials of Gorgon blood. One vial could raise the dead, the other was the deadliest poison ever known. "No, Aunt," he said. "I need only the first vial. You keep the other."

Some say that it was by his own skill that he restored life to the dead, and that Athene was simply trying to take some of the credit for herself. Be that as it may, he did snatch several patients from the very gates of Tartarus, and Hades was enraged. He complained to his brother Zeus that Asclepius was robbing him. Zeus stood on Olympus, hurled a thunderbolt, and killed the young physician together with the patient he was tending.

When Apollo heard about this, he went into one of his wild heedless rages, stormed to Olympus, battered in the doors of Hephaestus' smithy, and there slew all the Cyclopes, who had forged the thunderbolt which had killed his son. When Zeus heard this, he banished Apollo to Tartarus forever. But Mother Leto came and pleaded with him, reminding him of their old love. She spoke so beautifully that Zeus relented, withdrew the edict of Apollo's banishment, and even agreed to bring Asclepius back to life. But he suggested that Asclepius be more tactful about his cures and avoid offending the gods.

When Aphrodite heard this story, she was bitten by envy. She considered herself a favorite of Zeus, but he had never done so much for her. Her heart was bitter against Apollo, and she wanted to do him a mischief. She called her son Eros, the infant archer, whose sweetly poisoned arrows infect man and woman with a most dangerous fever. She told him what she wanted.

Eros had two kinds of arrows: one tipped with gold and tailed with white dove feathers—these were for love. The others, made of lead, with brown owl feathers, were the arrows of indifference. He took up his bow and stalked his game.

Apollo, he knew, was hunting; so he made Apollo's path cross that of Daphne, a mountain nymph, daughter of the river god, Penaeus. Then, fluttering above them, invisible, he shot Apollo with the dart of love and Daphne with the arrow of indifference. When the golden god came running down the slope toward the nymph, he saw her start up and run away. He could not understand it. She fled; the god pursued. She was a very swift runner, but great footsteps pounded behind her, and she felt the heat of his breath on her shoulders.

She ran toward the river and cried, "Oh, Father, save me! Save me!" Her father heard. Apollo, reaching for her, found himself hugging a tree; the rough bark scratched his face. He said, "But why?—why do you hate me so?"

The wind blew through the leaves, and they whispered, "I don't know. . . . I don't know. . . ."

But then the tree took pity on the grieving god and gave him a gift—a wreath of her leaves, laurel leaves that would never wither—to crown heroes and poets and young men who win games.

And still today, when questioned by losers, laurel trees whisper, "I don't know. . . . I don't know. . . ."

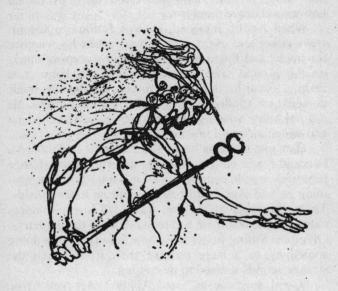

Hermes

Young gods were often precocious, but no one so much as Hermes who, five minutes after his birth, sneaked out of his crib and went searching for adventure. He toddled swiftly down the slope of Mount Cyllene until he came to a meadow where he saw a herd of beautiful white cows grazing. He saw no cowherd and decided to steal them. A treeful of crows began to seethe and whistle, "They belong to Apollo . . . to Apollo . . .

43

'pollo . . ." but he paid them no heed. He plaited grass into shoes for the cows and fitted them over their hooves and drove them away.

When Apollo returned, he was furious to see his cows gone, and even more furious when he searched for tracks and found none—only odd sweeping marks on the ground. The crows chattered, "A baby stole them . . . your brother, your brother . . ." But this made no sense to Apollo; besides he did not trust crows. He did not know where to begin looking; he searched far and wide, but could find no clue.

Then one morning he passed a cave he had passed a hundred times before. But this time he heard strange beautiful sounds coming out of it—sounds unlike anything he had ever heard before—and he looked inside. There, drowsing by the fire, was a tall lovely Titaness named Maia, whom he had seen before in the garden on Olympus. Sitting in her lap was a little baby boy doing something to a large tortoise shell from which the strange sounds seemed to be coming.

"Good day, cousin," said Apollo. "Are you to be congratulated on a new son?"

"Hail, bright Phoebus," said Maia. "May I have the honor of presenting your half-brother, young Hermes?"

"Half-brother, eh? Well, that's an honor without being a distinction. What's that he's playing with?"

"He makes his own toys," said Maia proudly. "He's so clever, you can't imagine. He made this out of an old shell that he strung with cowgut, and from it he draws the most ravishing sounds. Listen—"

"Cowgut? May I ask what cow he persuaded to contribute her vital cords for his pastime?"

"I do not understand your question, cousin."

"Understand this, cousin. I have had a herd of cows stolen recently. The crows told me they had been taken by some baby, my brother, but I didn't believe them. I seem to owe them an apology."

"What?" cried Maia. "Are you accusing the innocent babe of being a cattle thief? For shame!"

"Mother, if you don't mind," said a clear little voice, "perhaps you'd better let me handle this." The baby stood on his mother's knee and bowed to Apollo. "I did take your cows, brother. But I didn't know they were yours. How could I have? And they are quite safe, except for one. Wishing to begin my life with an act of piety, I sacrificed her to the twelve gods."

"Twelve gods?" said Apollo haughtily. "I am acquainted with but eleven."

"Yes, sir," said Hermes. "But I have the honor to be the twelfth. Above all things, I wish your good will, fair brother. So, in return for this cow, allow me to make you a present—this instrument. I call it a lyre. I'll be glad to teach you to play."

Apollo was enchanted with the trade. He stayed in the cave all that afternoon practicing his scales. As he was strumming his new toy, he noticed Hermes cutting reeds, which the child swiftly tied together, notched in a certain way, then put to his lips, and began to make other sounds, even more beautiful than the lyre could produce.

"What's that?" cried Apollo. "What do you call that? I want that too."

"I don't need any more cows," said Hermes.

"I must have it. What else of mine do you wish?"

"Your golden staff."

"But this is my herdsman's staff. Do you not know that I am the god of herdsmen, and that this is the rod of authority?"

"A minor office," said Hermes. "Unworthy of the lord of the sun. Perhaps you would allow me to take over the chore. Give me your golden staff, and I will give you these pipes."

"Agreed! Agreed!"

"But since pipes and lyre together will make you god of music, I must have something to boot. Teach me augury."

"You drive a hard bargain for a nursling," said Apollo. "I think you belong on Olympus, brother. This cave will not long offer scope for your talents."

"Oh, yes, take me there!" cried Hermes. "I am eager to meet Father Zeus."

So Apollo took Hermes to Olympus and introduced him to his father. Zeus was intrigued by the wit and impudence of the child. He hid him away from Hera and spent hours conversing with him.

"You say you wish to enter the Pantheon," said Zeus. "But really—all the realms and powers seem to have been parceled out."

"Father, I am of modest nature," said Hermes. "I require no vast dignities. Only a chance to be useful, to serve you, and to dwell in your benign and potent presence. Let me be your herald. Let me carry your tidings. You will find me quick and resourceful, and what I can't remember I will make up. And, I guarantee, your subjects will get the message."

"Very well," said Zeus. "I will give you a trial."

So Hermes became the messenger god and accomplished his duties with such swiftness, ingenuity, and cheerfulness that he became a favorite of his father, who soon rewarded him with other posts. Hermes became patron of liars and thieves and gamblers, god of commerce, framer of treaties, and guardian of travelers. Hades became his client too and called upon him to usher the newly dead from earth to Tartarus.

He kept a workshop on Olympus and there invented the alphabet, astronomy, and the scales; also, playing cards and card games. He carried Apollo's golden staff decorated with white ribbons, wore a pot-shaped hat, and winged sandals which carried him through the air more swiftly than any bird could fly.

It was he who gave Zeus the idea of disguising himself and mingling with mortals when bored with Olympus. He joined his father in this, and they had many adventures together . . . which will be told in their place.

Hephaestus

No one celebrated the birth of Hephaestus. His mother, Hera, had awaited him with great eagerness, hoping for a child so beautiful, so gifted, that it would make Zeus forget his heroic swarm of children from lesser consorts. But when the baby was born, she was appalled to see that he was shriveled and ugly, with an irritating bleating wail. She did not wait for Zeus to see him, but snatched the infant up and hurled him off Olympus.

For a night and a day he fell, and hit the ground at the edge of the sea with such force that both of his legs were broken. He lay there on the beach mewing piteously, unable to crawl, wracked with pain, but unable to die because he was immortal. Finally the tide came up. A huge wave curled him under its arm and carried him off to sea. And there he sank like a stone, and was caught by the playful Thetis, a naiad, who thought he was a tadpole.

When Thetis understood it was a baby she had caught, she made a pet of him and kept him in her grotto. She was amazed at the way the crippled child worked shells and bright pebbles into jewelry. One day she appeared at a great festival of the gods, wearing a necklace he had made. Hera noticed the ornament and praised it and asked her how she had come by it. Thetis told her of the strange twisted child whom someone had dropped into the ocean, and who lived now in her cave making wonderful jewels. Hera divined that it was her own son and demanded him back.

Hephaestus returned to Olympus. There Hera presented him with a broken mountain nearby, where he could set up forges and bellows. She gave him the brawny Cyclopes to be his helpers, and promised him Aphrodite as a bride if he would labor in the mountain and make her fine things. Hephaestus agreed because he loved her and excused her cruelty to him.

"I know that I am ugly, Mother," he said, "but the fates would have it so. And I will make you gems so beautiful for your tapering arms and white throat and black hair that you will forget my ugliness sometimes, and rejoice that you have taken me back from the sea."

He became the smith-god, the great artificer, lord of mechanics. And the mountain always smoked and rumbled with his toil, and he has always been very ugly and very useful.

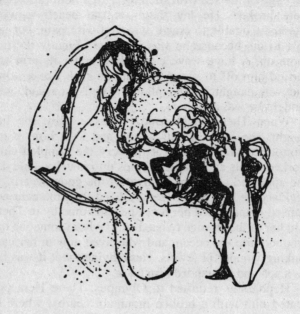

Aphrodite

Aphrodite was the goddess of love and beauty; so there are more stories told about her than anyone else, god or mortal. Being what she is, she enters other stories; and such is the power of her magic girdle that he who even speaks her name falls under her spell, and seems to glimpse her white shoulders and catch the perfume of her golden hair. And he loses his wits and begins to babble and tells the same story in many ways.

But all the tales agree that she is the goddess of desire, and, unlike other Olympians, is never distracted from her duties. Her work is her pleasure; her profession, her hobby. She thinks of nothing but love, and nobody expects more of her.

She was born out of the primal murder. When Cronos butchered his father, Oranos, with the scythe his mother had given him, he flung the dismembered body off Olympus into the sea, where it floated, spouting blood and seed which drifted, whitening in the sun. From the foam rose a tall beautiful maiden, naked and dripping. Waves attended her. Poseidon's white horses brought her to the island of Cythera. Wherever she stepped, the sand turned to grass and flowers bloomed. Then she went to Cyprus. Hillsides burst into flowers, and the air was full of birds.

Zeus brought her to Olympus. She was still dripping from the sea. She wore nothing but the bright tunic of her hair, which fell to mid-thigh and was yellow as daffodils. She looked about the great throne room where the gods were assembled to meet her, arched her throat, and laughed with joy.

Hera was watching Zeus narrowly. "You must marry her off," she whispered. "At once—without delay!"

"Yes," said Zeus. "Some sort of marriage would seem to be indicated."

And he said, "Brothers, sons, cousins, Aphrodite is to be married. She will choose her own husband. So make your suit."

The gods closed around her, shouting promises, pressing their claims. Earth-shaking Poseidon swung his mighty trident to clear a space about himself. "I claim you for the sea," he said. "You are sea-born, foam-born, and belong to me. I offer you grottoes, riddles, gems, fair surfaces, dark surroundings. I offer you variety. Drowned sailors, typhoons, sunsets. I offer you secrets. I offer you riches that the earth does not know—power more subtle, more fluid than the dull fixed land. Come with me—be queen of the sea."

He slammed his trident on the floor, and a huge green tidal wave swelled out of the sea—high, high as Olympus, curling its mighty green tongue as if to lick up the mountain—and poised there, quivering, not breaking, as the gods gaped. Then Poseidon raised his trident, and the mighty wave subsided like a ripple. He bowed to Aphrodite. She smiled at him, but said nothing.

Then the gods spoke in turn, offering her great gifts. Apollo offered her a throne and a crown made of hottest sun-gold, a golden chariot drawn by white swans, and the Muses for her handmaids. Hermes offered to make her queen of the crossways where all must come—where she would hear every story, see every traveler, know each deed—a rich pageant of adventure and gossip so that she would never grow bored.

She smiled at Apollo and Hermes and made no answer.

Then Hera, scowling, reached her long white arm and dragged Hephaestus, the lame smith-god, from where he had been hiding behind the others, ashamed to be seen. And she hissed into his ear, "Speak, fool. Say exactly what I told you to say."

He limped forward with great embarrassment and stood before the radiant goddess, eyes cast down, not daring to look at her. He said, "I would make a good husband for a girl like you. I work late."

Aphrodite smiled. She said nothing, but put her finger under the chin of the grimy little smith, raised his face, leaned down, and kissed him on the lips.

That night they were married. And at the wedding party she finally spoke—whispering to each of her suitors—telling each one when he might come with his gift.

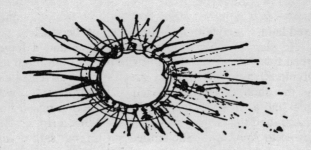

NATURE MYTHS

Prometheus

Prometheus was a young Titan, no great admirer of Zeus. Although he knew the great lord of the sky hated explicit questions, he did not hesitate to beard him when there was something he wanted to know.

One morning he came to Zeus, and said, "O Thunderer, I do not understand your design. You have caused the race of man to appear on earth, but you keep him in ignorance and darkness."

"Perhaps you had better leave the race of man to me," said Zeus. "What you call ignorance is innocence. What you call darkness is the shadow of my decree. Man is happy now. And he is so framed that he will remain happy unless someone persuades him that he is unhappy. Let us not speak of this again."

But Prometheus said, "Look at him. Look below. He crouches in caves. He is at the mercy of beast and weather. He eats his meat raw. If you mean something by this, enlighten me with your wisdom. Tell me why you refuse to give man the gift of fire."

Zeus answered, "Do you not know, Prometheus, that every gift brings a penalty? This is the way the Fates weave destiny—by which gods also must abide. Man does not have fire, true, nor the crafts which fire teaches. On the other hand, he does not know disease, warfare, old age, or that inward pest called worry. He is happy, I say, happy without fire. And so he shall remain."

"Happy as beasts are happy," said Prometheus. "Of what use to make a separate race called man and endow him with little fur, some wit, and a curious charm of unpredictability? If he must live like this, why separate him from the beasts at all?"

"He has another quality," said Zeus, "the capacity for worship. An aptitude for admiring our power, being puzzled by our riddles and amazed by our caprice. That is why he was made."

"Would not fire, and the graces he can put on with fire, make him more interesting?"

"More interesting, perhaps, but infinitely more dangerous. For there is this in man too: a vaunting pride that needs little sustenance to make it swell to giant size. Improve his lot, and he will forget that which makes him pleasing—his sense of worship, his humility. He will grow big and poisoned with pride and fancy himself a god, and before we know it, we shall see him storming Olympus. Enough, Prometheus! I have been patient with you, but do not try me too far. Go now and trouble me no more with your speculations."

Prometheus was not satisfied. All that night he lay awake making plans. Then he left his couch at dawn, and standing tiptoe on Olympus, stretched his arm to the eastern horizon where the first faint flames of the sun were flickering. In his hand he held a reed filled with a dry fiber; he thrust it into the sunrise until a spark smoldered. Then he put the reed in his tunic and came down from the mountain.

At first men were frightened by the gift. It was so hot, so quick; it bit sharply when you touched it, and for pure spite, made the shadows dance. They thanked Prometheus and asked him to take it away. But he took the haunch of a newly killed deer and held it over the fire. And when the meat began to sear and sputter, filling the cave with its rich smells, the people felt themselves melting with hunger and flung themselves on the meat and devoured it greedily, burning their tongues.

"This that I have brought you is called 'fire,' " Prometheus said. "It is an ill-natured spirit, a little brother of the sun, but if you handle it carefully, it can change your whole life. It is very greedy; you must feed it twigs, but only until it becomes a proper size. Then you must stop, or it will eat everything in sight—and you too. If it escapes, use this magic: water. It fears the water spirit, and if you touch it with water, it will fly away until you need it again."

He left the fire burning in the first cave, with children staring at it wide-eyed, and then went to every cave in the land.

Then one day Zeus looked down from the mountain and was amazed. Everything had changed. Man had come out of his cave. Zeus saw woodmen's huts, farm houses, villages, walled towns, even a castle or two. He saw men cooking their food, carrying torches to light their way at night. He saw forges blazing, men beating out ploughs, keels, swords, spears. They were making ships and raising white wings of sails and daring to use the fury of the winds for their journeys. They were wearing helmets, riding out in chariots to do battle, like the gods themselves.

Zeus was full of rage. He seized his largest thunderbolt. "So they want fire," he said to himself. "I'll give them fire—more than they can use. I'll turn their miserable little ball of earth into a cinder." But then another thought came to him, and he lowered his arm. "No," he said to himself, "I shall have vengeance—and entertainment too. Let them destroy themselves with their new skills. This will make a long twisted game, interesting to watch. I'll attend to them later. My first business is with Prometheus."

He called his giant guards and had them seize Prometheus, drag him off to the Caucasus, and there bind him to a mountain peak with great chains specially forged by Hephaestus—chains which even a Titan in agony could not break. And when the friend of man was bound to the mountain, Zeus sent two vultures to hover about him forever, tearing at his belly and eating his liver.

Men knew a terrible thing was happening on the mountain, but they did not know what. But the wind shrieked like a giant in torment and sometimes like fierce birds.

Many centuries he lay there—until another hero was born brave enough to defy the gods. He climbed to the peak in the Caucasus and struck the shackles from Prometheus and killed the vultures. His name was Heracles.

Pandora

After Zeus had condemned Prometheus for giving fire to man, he began to plan how to punish man for accepting it.

Finally he hit upon a scheme. He ordered Hephaestus to mold a girl out of clay and to have Aphrodite pose for it to make sure it was beautiful. He breathed life into the clay figure; the clay turned to flesh, and she lay sleeping, all new. Then he summoned the gods and asked them each to give her a gift.

Apollo taught her to sing and play the lyre. Athene taught her to spin, Demeter to tend a garden. Aphrodite taught her how to look at a man without moving her eyes and how to dance without moving her legs. Poseidon gave her a pearl necklace and promised she would never drown. And finally Hermes gave her a beautiful golden box, which, he told her, she must never, never open. And then Hera gave her curiosity.

Hermes took her by the hand and led her down the slope of Olympus. He led her to Epimetheus, brother of Prometheus, and said, "Father Zeus grieves at the disgrace which has fallen upon your family. And to show you that he holds you blameless in your brother's offense, he makes you this gift—this girl, fairest in all the world. She is to be your wife. Her name is Pandora, the all-gifted."

So Epimetheus and Pandora were married. Pandora spun and baked and tended her garden, and played the lyre and danced for her husband, and thought herself the happiest young bride in all the world. Only one thing bothered her—the golden box. First she kept it on the table and polished it every day so that all might admire it. But the sunlight lanced through the window, and the box sparkled and seemed to be winking at her.

She found herself thinking, "Hermes must have been teasing. He's always making jokes; everyone knows that. Yes, he was teasing, telling me never to open his gift. For if it is so beautiful outside, what must it be inside? Why, he has hidden a surprise for me there. Gems more lovely than have ever been seen, no doubt. If the box is so rich, the gift inside must be even more splendid—for that is the way of gifts. Perhaps Hermes is *waiting* for me to open the box and see what is inside and be delighted and thank him. Perhaps he thinks me ungrateful . . ."

But even as she was telling herself this, she knew it

was not so—that the box must not be opened, that she must keep her promise.

Finally she took the box from the table and hid it in a dusty little storeroom. But it seemed to be burning there in the shadows. Its heat seemed to scorch her thoughts wherever she went. She kept passing that room and stepping into it, making excuses to dawdle there. Sometimes she took the box from its hiding place and stroked it, then quickly shoved it out of sight, and rushed out of the room.

She took it then, locked it in a heavy oaken chest, put great shackles on the chest, and dug a hole in her garden. She put the chest in, covered it over, and rolled a boulder on top of it. When Epimetheus came home that night, her hair was wild and her hands were bloody, her tunic torn and stained. But all she would tell him was that she had been working in the garden.

That night the moonlight blazed into the room. She could not sleep. The light pressed her eyes open. She sat up in bed and looked around. All the room was swimming in moonlight. Everything was different. There were deep shadows and swaths of silver, all mixed, all moving. She arose quietly and tiptoed from the room.

She went out into the garden. The flowers were blowing, the trees were swaying. The whole world was adance in the magic white fire of that moonlight. She walked to the rock and pushed it. It rolled away as lightly as a pebble. And she felt herself full of wild strength.

She took a shovel and dug down to the chest. She unshackled it and drew out the golden box. It was cold, cold; coldness burned her hand to the bone. She trembled. What was inside that box seemed to her now the very secret of life, which she must look upon or die.

She took the little golden key from her tunic, fitted it

into the keyhole, and gently opened the lid. There was a swarming, a hot throbbing, a wild meaty rustling, and a foul smell. Out of the box, as she held it up in the moonlight, swarmed small scaly lizardlike creatures with bat wings and burning red eyes.

They flew out of the box, circled her head once, clapping their wings and screaming thin little jeering screams—and then flew off into the night, hissing and cackling.

Then, half-fainting, sinking to her knees, Pandora, with her last bit of strength, clutched the box and slammed down the lid—catching the last little monster just as it was wriggling free. It shrieked and spat and clawed her hand, but she thrust it back into the box and locked it in. Then she dropped the box and fainted away.

What were those deathly creatures that flew out of the golden box? They were the ills that beset mankind: the spites, disease in its thousand shapes, old age, famine, insanity, and all their foul kin. After they flew out of the box, they scattered—flew into every home and swung from the rafters—waiting. And when their time comes, they fly and sting—and bring pain and sorrow and death.

At that, things could have been much worse. For the creature that Pandora shut into the box was the most dangerous of all. It was Foreboding, the final spite. If it had flown free, everyone in the world would have been told exactly what misfortune was to happen every day of his life. No hope would have been possible. And so there would have been an end to man. For though he can bear endless trouble, he cannot live with no hope at all.

Phaethon

Long ago, when the world was very new, two boys were racing along the edge of a cliff that hung over a deep blue sea. They were the same size; one boy had black hair, the other had yellow hair. The race was very close. Then the yellow-haired one spurted ahead and won the race. The loser was very angry.

"You think you're pretty good," he said. "But you're not so much. My father is Zeus."

"My father is Apollo," said the yellow-haired boy, whose name was Phaethon.

"My father is the chief god, king of the mountain, lord of the sky."

"My father is lord of the sun."

"My father is called the thunderer. When he is angry, the sky grows black and the sun hides. His spear is a lightning bolt, and that's what he kills people with. He hurls it a thousand miles and it never misses."

"Without my father there would be no day. It would always be night. Each morning he hitches up his horses and drives the golden chariot of the sun across the sky. And that is day time. Then he dives into the ocean stream and boards a golden ferryboat and sails back to his eastern palace. That time is called night."

"Sometimes I visit my father," said Epaphus, the other boy. "I sit on Olympus with him, and he teaches me things and gives me presents. Know what he gave me last time? A little thunderbolt just like his—and he taught me how to throw it. I killed three vultures, scared a fishing boat, started a forest fire. Next time I go, I'll throw it at more things. Do you visit your father?"

Phaethon never had. But he could not bear to tell Epaphus. "Certainly," he said, "very often. I go to the eastern palace, and he teaches me things too."

"What kind of things? Has he taught you to drive the horses of the sun?"

"Oh, yes. He taught me to handle their reins and how to make them go and how to make them stop. And they're huge horses. Tall as this mountain. They breathe fire."

"I think you're making it all up," said Epaphus. "I can tell. I don't even believe there is a sun chariot. There's the sun, look at it. It's not a chariot."

"Oh, what you see is just one of the wheels," said Phaethon. "There's another wheel on the other side.

The body of the chariot is slung between them. That is where the driver stands and whips his horses. You cannot see it because your eyes are too small, and the glare is too bright."

"Well," said Epaphus. "Maybe it is a chariot, but I still don't believe your father lets you drive it. In fact, I don't believe you've been to the palace of the sun. I doubt that Apollo would know you if he saw you. Maybe he isn't even your father. People like to say they're descended from the gods, of course. But how many of us are there, really?"

"I'll prove it to you," cried Phaethon, stamping his foot. "I'll go to the palace of the sun right now and hold my father to his promise. I'll show you."

"What promise?"

"He said I was getting to be so good a charioteer that next time he would let me drive the sun chariot *alone*. All by myself. From dawn to night. Right across the sky. And this time is next time."

"Poof—words are cheap," said Epaphus. "How will I know it's you driving the sun? I won't be able to see you from down here."

"You'll know me," said Phaethon. "When I pass the village I will come down close and drive in circles around your roof. You'll see me all right. Farewell."

"Are you starting now?"

"Now. At once. Just watch the sky tomorrow, son of Zeus."

And he went off. He was so stung by the words of his friend, and the boasting and lying he had been forced to do, that he traveled night and day, not stopping for food or rest, guiding himself by the morning star and the evening star, heading always east. Nor did he know the way. For, indeed, he had never once seen his father Apollo. He knew him only through his mother's stories. But he did know that the palace must lie in the east, because that is where he saw the sun start each morning. He walked on and on until finally he lost his way completely, and weakened by hunger and exhaustion, fell swooning in a great meadow by the edge of a wood.

Now, while Phaethon was making his journey, Apollo sat in his great throne room on a huge throne made of gold and rubies. This was the quiet hour before dawn when night left its last coolness upon the earth. And it was then, at this hour, that Apollo sat on his throne, wearing a purple cloak embroidered with the golden signs of the zodiac. On his head was a crown given him by the dawn goddess, made of silver and pearls. A bird flew in the window and perched on his shoulder and spoke to him. This bird had sky-blue feathers, golden beak, golden claws, and golden eyes. It was one of Apollo's sun hawks. It was this bird's job to fly here and there gathering gossip. Sometimes she was called the spy bird.

Now she said, "Apollo, I have seen your son!"

"Which son?"

"Phaethon. He's coming to see you. But he has lost his way and lies exhausted at the edge of the wood. The wolves will surely eat him. Do you care?"

"I will have to see him before I know whether I care. You had better get back to him before the wolves do. Bring him here in comfort. Round up some of your companions and bring him here as befits the son of a god."

The sun hawk seized the softly glowing rug at the foot of the throne and flew away with it. She summoned three of her companions, and they each took a corner of the rug. They flew over a desert and a mountain and a wood and came to the field where Phaethon lay. They flew down among the howling of wolves, among burning eyes set in a circle about the unconscious boy. They pushed him onto the rug, and each took a corner in her beak, and flew away.

Phaethon felt himself being lifted into the air. The cold wind of his going revived him, and he sat up. People below saw a boy sitting with folded arms on a carpet rushing through the cold, bright moonlight far above their heads. It was too dark, though, to see the birds, and that is why we hear tales of flying carpets even to this day.

Phaethon was not particularly surprised to find himself in the air. The last thing he remembered was lying down on the grass. Now, he knew, he was dreaming. A good dream—floating and flying—his favorite kind. And when he saw the great cloud castle on top of the mountain, all made of snow, rose in the early light, he was more sure than ever that he was dreaming. He saw sentries in flashing golden armor, carrying golden spears. In the courtyard he saw enormous woolly dogs with fleece like clouddrift guarding the gate. These were Apollo's great sun hounds.

Over the wall flew the carpet, over the courtyard, through the tall portals. And it wasn't until the sun hawks gently let down the carpet in front of the throne that he began to think that this dream might be very real. He raised his eyes shyly and saw a tall figure sitting on the throne. Taller than any man, and appallingly beautiful to the boy—with his golden hair and stormy blue eyes and strong laughing face. Phaethon fell on his knees.

"Father," he cried. "I am Phaethon, your son!"

"Rise, Phaethon. Let me look at you."

He stood up, his legs trembling.

"Yes, you may well be my son. I seem to see a resemblance. Which one did you say?"

"Phaethon."

"Oh, Clymene's boy. I remember your mother well. How is she?"

"In health, sire."

"And did I not leave some daughters with her as well? Yellow-haired girls—quite pretty?"

"My sisters, sire. The Heliads."

"Yes, of course. Must get over that way and visit them all one of these seasons. And you, lad—what brings you to me? Do you not know that it is courteous to await an invitation before visiting a god—even if he is in the family?"

"I know, Father. But I had no choice. I was taunted by a son of Zeus, Epaphus. And I would have flung him over the cliff and myself after him if I had not resolved to make my lies come true."

"Well, you're my son, all right. Proud, rash, accepting no affront, refusing no adventure. I know the breed. Speak up, then. What is it you wish? I will do anything in my power to help you."

"Anything, Father?"

"Anything I can. I swear by the river Styx, an oath sacred to the gods."

"I wish to drive the sun across the sky. All by myself. From dawn till night."

Apollo's roar of anger shattered every crystal goblet in the great castle.

"Impossible!" he cried. "No one drives those horses but me. They are tall as mountains. Their breath is fire. They are stronger than the tides, stronger than the wind. It is all that *I* can do to hold them in check. How can your puny grip restrain them? They will race away with the chariot, scorching the poor earth to a cinder."

"You promised, Father."

"Yes, I promised, foolish lad. And that promise is a death warrant. A poor charred cinder floating in space—well, that is what the oracle predicted for the earth—but I did not know it would be so soon . . . so soon."

"It is almost dawn, Father. Should we not saddle the horses?"

"Will you not withdraw your request—allow me to

preserve my honor without destroying the earth? Ask me anything else and I will grant it. Do not ask me this."

"I have asked, sire, and you have promised. And the hour for dawn comes, and the horses are unharnessed. The sun will rise late today, confusing the wise."

"They will be more than confused when this day is done," said Apollo. "Come."

Apollo took Phaethon to the stable of the sun, and there the boy saw the giant fire-white horses being harnessed to the golden chariot. Huge they were. Fire-white with golden manes and golden hooves and hot yellow eyes. When they neighed, the trumpet call of it rolled across the sky—and their breath was flame. They were being harnessed by a Titan, a cousin of the gods, tall as a tree, dressed in asbestos armor with helmet of tinted crystal against the glare. The sun chariot was an open shell of gold. Each wheel was the flat round disk of the sun as it is seen in the sky. And Phaethon looked very tiny as he stood in the chariot. The reins were thick as bridge cables, much too large for him to hold, so Apollo tied them around his waist. Then Apollo stood at the head of the team gentling the horses, speaking softly to them, calling them by name—Pyroeis, Eous, Aethon, Phlegon.

"Good lads, good horses, go easy today, my swift ones. Go at a slow trot and do not leave the path. You have a new driver today."

The great horses dropped their heads to his shoulder and whinnied softly, for they loved him. Phaethon saw the flame of their breath play about his head, saw Apollo's face shining out of the flame. But he was not harmed, for he was a god and could not be hurt by physical things.

He came to Phaethon and said, "Listen to me, son. You are about to start a terrible journey. Now, by the

obedience you owe me as a son, by the faith you owe a
god, by my oath that cannot be broken, and your pride
that will not bend, I put this rule upon you: Keep the
middle way. Too high and the earth will freeze, too low
and it will burn. Keep the middle way. Give the horses
their heads; they know the path, the blue middle course
of day. Drive them not too high nor too low, but above
all, do not stop. Or you will fire the air about you where
you stand, charring the earth and blistering the sky. Do
you heed me?"

"I do, I do!" cried Phaethon. "Stand away, sire! The
dawn grows old and day must begin! Go, horses, go!"

And Apollo stood watching as the horses of the sun
went into a swinging trot, pulling behind them the
golden chariot, climbing the first eastern steep of the
sky.

At first things went well. The great steeds trotted
easily along their path across the high blue meadow of
the sky. And Phaethon thought to himself, "I can't understand why my father was making such a fuss. This
is easy. For me, anyway. Perhaps I'm a natural-born
coachman though . . ."

He looked over the edge of the chariot. He saw tiny
houses down below and specks of trees. And the dark
blue puddle of the sea. The coach was trundling across
the sky. The great sun wheels were turning, casting
light, warming and brightening the earth, chasing all
the shadows of night.

"Just imagine," Phaethon thought, "how many people now are looking up at the sky, praising the sun, hoping the weather stays fair. How many people are
watching me, me, me . . . ?" Then he thought, "But I'm
too small to see. They can't even see the coach or the
horses—only the great wheel. We are too far and the
light is too bright. For all they know, it is Apollo making his usual run. How can they know it's me, me, me?

How will my mother know, and my sisters? They would be so proud. And Epaphus—above all, Epaphus—how will *he* know? I'll come home tomorrow after this glorious journey and tell him what I did and he will laugh at me and tell me I'm lying, as he did before. And how shall I prove it to him? No, this must not be. I must show him that it is I driving the chariot of the sun—I alone. Apollo said not to come too close to earth, but how will he know? And I won't stay too long—just dip down toward our own village and circle his roof three times—which is the signal we agreed upon. After he recognizes me, I'll whip up the horses and resume the path of the day."

He jerked on the reins, pulled the horses' heads down. They whinnied angrily and tossed their heads. He jerked the reins again.

"Down," he cried. "Down! Down!"

The horses plunged through the bright air, golden hooves twinkling, golden manes flying, dragging the great glittering chariot after them in a long flaming swoop. When they reached his village, he was horrified to see the roofs bursting into fire. The trees burned. People rushed about screaming. Their loose clothing caught fire, and they burned like torches as they ran.

Was it his village? He could not tell because of the smoke. Had he destroyed his own home? Burned his mother and his sisters?

He threw himself backward in the chariot, pulling at the reins with all his might, shouting, "Up! Up!"

And the horses, made furious by the smoke, reared on their hind legs in the air. Then leaped upward, galloping through the smoke, pulling the chariot up, up.

Swiftly the earth fell away beneath them. The village was just a smudge of smoke. Again he saw the pencilstroke of mountains, the inkblot of seas. "Whoa!" he cried. "Turn now! Forward on your path!" But he

could no longer handle them. They were galloping, not
trotting. They had taken the bit in their teeth. They did
not turn toward the path of the day across the meadow
of the sky, but galloped up, up. And the people on earth
saw the sun shooting away until it was no larger than a
star.

Darkness came. And cold. The earth froze hard.
Rivers froze, and oceans. Boats were caught fast in the
ice in every sea. It snowed in the jungle. Marble build-
ings cracked. It was impossible for anyone to speak;
breath froze on the speakers' lips. And in village and
city, in the field and in the wood, people died of the
cold. And the bodies piled up where they fell, like fire-
wood.

Still Phaethon could not hold his horses, and still
they galloped upward dragging light and warmth away
from the earth. Finally they went so high that the air
was too thin to breathe. Phaethon saw the flame of their
breath, which had been red and yellow, burn blue in the
thin air. He himself was gasping for breath; he felt the
marrow of his bones freezing.

Now the horses, wild with change, maddened by the
feeble hand on the reins, swung around and dived toward earth again. Now all the ice melted, making great
floods. Villages were swept away by a solid wall of
water. Trees were uprooted and whole forests were
torn away. The fields were covered by water. Lower
swooped the horses, and lower yet. Now the water began to steam—great billowing clouds of steam as the
water boiled. Dead fish floated on the surface. Naiads
moaned in dry riverbeds.

Phaethon could not see; the steam was too thick. He
had unbound the reins from his waist, or they would
have cut him in two. He had no control over the horses
at all. They galloped upward again—out of the steam—
taking at last the middle road, but racing wildly, using

all their tremendous speed. Circling the earth in a matter of minutes, smashing across the sky from horizon to horizon, making the day flash on and off like a child playing with a lamp. And the people who were left alive were bewildered by the light and darkness following each other so swiftly.

Up high on Olympus, the gods in their cool garden heard a clamor of grief from below. Zeus looked upon earth. He saw the runaway horses of the sun and the hurtling chariot. He saw the dead and the dying, the burning forests, the floods, the weird frost. Then he looked again at the chariot and saw that it was not Apollo driving but someone he did not know. He stood up, drew back his arm, and hurled a thunderbolt.

It stabbed through the air, striking Phaethon, killing him instantly, knocking him out of the chariot. His body, flaming, fell like a star. And the horses of the sun, knowing themselves driverless, galloped homeward toward their stables at the eastern edge of the sky.

Phaethon's yellow-haired sisters grieved for the beautiful boy. They could not stop weeping. They stood on the bank of the river where he had fallen until Apollo, unable to comfort them, changed them into poplar trees. Here they still stand on the shore of the river, weeping tears of amber sap.

And since that day no one has been allowed to drive the chariot of the sun except the sun god himself. But there are still traces of Phaethon's ride. The ends of the earth are still covered with icecaps. Mountains still rumble, trying to spit out the fire started in their bellies by the diving sun.

Orpheus

His father was a Thracian king; his mother, the Muse, Calliope. For awhile he lived on Parnassus with his mother and his eight beautiful aunts and there met Apollo, who was courting the laughing Muse, Thalia. Apollo was taken with Orpheus and gave him a little golden lyre and taught him to play. And his mother taught him to make verses for singing.

So he grew up to be a poet and musician such as the

world had never known. Fishermen used to coax him to go sailing with them early in the morning and had him play his lyre on the deck. They knew that the fish would come up from the depths of the sea to hear him and sit on their tails and listen as he played, making it easy to catch them. But they were not caught, for as soon as Orpheus began to play, the fishermen forgot all about their nets and sat on deck and listened with their mouths open—just like the fish. And when he had finished, the fish dived, the fishermen awoke, and all was as before.

When he played in the fields, animals followed him, sheep and cows and goats. And not only the tame animals but the wild ones too—the shy deer, and wolves, and bears. They all followed him, streaming across the fields, following him, listening. When he sat down, they would gather in a circle about him, listening. Nor did the bears and wolves think of eating the sheep until the music had stopped, and it was too late. And they went off growling to themselves about the chance they had missed.

And as he grew and practiced, he played more and more beautifully, so that now not only animals but trees followed him as he walked, wrenching themselves out of the earth and hobbling after him on their twisted roots. In Thrace now there are circles of trees that still stand, listening.

People followed him too, of course, as he strolled about, playing and singing. Men and women, boys and girls—particularly girls. But as time passed and the faces changed he noticed that one face was always there. She was always there—in front, listening—when he played. She became especially noticeable because she began to appear among his other listeners, among the animals and the trees who listened as he played. So that finally he knew, that wherever he might be, wherever he might strike up his lyre and raise his voice in song, whether people were listening, or animals or trees and rocks—she would be there, very slender and still, with huge dark eyes and long black hair, her face like a rose.

Then one day he took her aside and spoke to her. Her name was Eurydice. She said she wanted to do nothing but be where he was, always; and that she knew she could not hope for him to love her, but that would not stop her from following him and serving him in any way she could. She would be happy to be his slave if he wanted her to.

Now, this is the kind of thing any man likes to hear in any age, particularly a poet. And although Orpheus was admired by many women and could have had his choice, he decided that he must have this one, so much like a child still, with her broken murmurs and great slavish eyes. And so he married her.

They lived happily, very happily, for a year and a day. They lived in a little house near the river in a grove of trees that pressed close, and they were so happy that they rarely left home. People began to wonder why Orpheus was never seen about, why his wonderful lyre was never heard. They began to gossip, as people do. Some said Orpheus was dead, killed by the jealous Apollo for playing so well. Others said he had fallen in love with a river nymph, had gone into the water after her, and now lived at the bottom of the river, coming up only at dawn to blow tunes upon the reeds that grew thickly near the shore. And others said that he had married dangerously, that he lived with a sorceress, who with her enchantments made herself so beautiful that he was chained to her side and would not leave her even for a moment.

It was the last rumor that people chose to believe. Among them was a visitor—Aristeus, a young king of

Athens, Apollo's son by the nymph Cyrene, and a mighty hunter. Aristeus decided that he must see this beautiful enchantress, and stationed himself in the grove of trees and watched the house. For two nights and two days he watched. Then finally he saw a girl come out. She made her way through the grove and went down the path toward the river. He followed. When he reached the river, he saw her there, taking off her tunic.

Without a word he charged toward her, crashing like a wild boar through the reeds. Eurydice looked up and saw a stranger hurtling toward her. She fled. Swiftly she ran—over the grass toward the trees. She heard him panting after her. She doubled back toward the river and ran, heedless of where she was going, wild to escape. And she stepped full on a nest of coiled and sleeping snakes, who awoke immediately and bit her leg in so many places that she was dead before she fell. And Aristeus, rushing up, found her lying in the reeds.

He left her body where he found it. There it lay until Orpheus, looking for her, came at dusk and saw her glimmering whitely like a fallen birch. By this time Hermes had come and gone, taking her soul with him to Tartarus. Orpheus stood looking down at her. He did not weep. He touched a string of his lyre once, absently, and it sobbed. But only once—he did not touch it again. He kept looking at her. She was pale and thin, her hair was disheveled, her legs streaked with mud. She seemed more childish than ever. He looked down at her, dissatisfied with the way she looked, as he felt when he set a wrong word in a verse. She was wrong this way. She did not belong dead. He would have to correct it. He turned abruptly and set off across the field.

He entered Tartarus at the nearest place, a passage in the mountains called Avernus, and walked through a cold mist until he came to the river Styx. He saw shades waiting there to be ferried across, but not Eurydice. She must have crossed before. The ferry came back and put out its plank, and the shades went on board, each one reaching under his tongue for the penny to pay the fare. But the ferryman, Charon, huge and swart and scowling, stopped Orpheus when he tried to embark.

"Stand off!" he cried. "Only the dead go here."

Orpheus touched his lyre and began to sing—a river song, a boat song, about streams running in the sunlight, and boys making twig boats, and then growing up to be young men who go in boats, and how they row down the river thrusting with powerful young arms, and what the water smells like in the morning when you are young, and the sound of oars dipping.

And Charon, listening, felt himself carried back to his own youth—to the time before he had been taken by Hades and put to work on the black river. And he was so lost in memory that the great sweep oar fell from his hand, and he stood there, dazed, tears streaming down his face—and Orpheus took up the oar and rowed across.

The shades filed off the ferry and through the gates of Tartarus. Orpheus followed them. Then he heard a hideous growling. An enormous dog with three heads, each one uglier than the next, slavered and snarled. It was the three-headed dog, Cerberus, who guarded the gates of Tartarus.

Orpheus unslung his lyre and played. He played a dog song, a hound song, a hunting song. In it was the faint far yapping of happy young hounds finding a fresh trail—dogs with one graceful head in the middle where it should be, dogs that run through the light and shade of the forest chasing stags and wolves, as dogs should do and are not forced to stand forever before dark gates, barking at ghosts.

Cerberus lay down and closed his six eyes, lolled his

three tongues, and went to sleep to dream of the days when he had been a real dog, before he had been captured and changed and trained as a sentinel for the dead. Orpheus stepped over him and went through the gates.

Through the Field of Aspholdel he walked, playing. The shades twittered thin glee, like bats giggling. Sisyphus stopped pushing his stone, and the stone itself poised on the side of the hill to listen and did not fall back. Tantalus heard and stopped lunging his head at the water; the music laved his thirst. Minos and Rhadamanthys and Aeacus, the great judges of the dead, heard the music on their high benches and fell dreaming about the old days on Crete where they had been young princes, about the land battles and the sea battles and the white bulls and the beautiful maidens and the flashing swords, and all the days gone by. They sat there, listening, eyes blinded with tears, deaf to litigants.

Then Hades, king of the underworld, lord of the dead, knowing his great proceedings disrupted, waited sternly on his throne as Orpheus approached.

"No more cheap minstrel tricks," he cried. "I am a god. My rages are not to be assuaged, nor my decrees nullified. No one comes to Tartarus without being sent for. No one has before, and no one will again, when the tale is told of the torments I intend to put you to."

Orpheus touched his lyre and sang a song that conjured up a green field and a grove of trees and a slender girl painting flowers and all the light about her head, with the special clearness there was when the world had just begun. He sang of how that girl made a sight so pleasing as she played with the flowers that the birds overhead gossiped of it, and the moles underground—until the word reached even gloomy Tartarus, where a dark king heard and went up to see for himself. Orpheus sang of that king seeing the girl for the first time in a great wash of early sunlight, and what he felt when he saw that stalk-slender child in her tunic and green shoes moving with her paintpot among the flowers; of the fever that ran in his blood when first he put his mighty arm about her waist, and drank her screams with his dark lips and tasted her tears; of the grief that had come upon him when he almost lost her again to her mother by Zeus's decree; and of the joy that filled him when he learned that she had eaten of the pomegranate.

Persephone was sitting at Hades' side. She began to cry. Hades looked at her. She leaned forward and whispered to him swiftly. The king turned to Orpheus. Hades did not weep, but no one had ever seen his eyes so brilliant.

"Your verse has affected my queen," he said. "Speak. We are disposed to hear. What is it you wish?"

"My wife."

"What have we to do with your wife?"

"She is here. She was brought here today. Her name is Eurydice. I wish to take her back with me."

"Never done," said Hades. "A disastrous precedent."

"Not so, great Hades," said Orpheus. "This one stroke of unique mercy will illumine like a lightning flash the caverns of your dread decree. Nature exists by proportion, and perceptions work by contrast, and the gods themselves are part of nature. This brilliant act of kindness, I say, will make cruelty seem like justice for all the rest of time. Pray give me back my wife again, great monarch. For I will not leave without her—not for all the torments that can be devised."

He touched his lyre once again, and the Eumenides, hearing the music, flew in on their hooked wings, their brass claws tinkling like bells, and poised in the air above Hades' throne. The terrible hags cooed like doves, saying, "Just this once, Hades. Let him have her. Let her go."

Hades stood up then, black-caped and towering. He

looked down at Orpheus and said, "I must leave the laurel leaves and the loud celebrations to my bright nephew Apollo. But I, even I, of such dour repute, can be touched by eloquence. Especially when it attracts such unlikely advocates. Hear me then, Orpheus. You may have your wife. She will be given into your care, and you will conduct her yourself from Tartarus to the upper light. But if during your journey, you look back once, only once—if for any reason whatever you turn your eyes from where you are headed and look back toward where you were—then my leniency is revoked, and Eurydice will be taken from you again, and forever. Go. . . ."

Orpheus bowed, once to Hades, once to Persephone, lifted his head and smiled a half-smile at the hovering Furies, turned and walked away. Hades gestured. And as Orpheus walked through the fields of Tartarus, Eurydice fell into step behind him. He did not see her. He thought she was there, he was sure she was there. He thought he could hear her footfall, but the black grass was thick; he could not be sure. But he thought he recognized her breathing—that faint sipping of breath he had heard so many nights near his ear; he thought he heard her breathing, but the air again was full of the howls of the tormented, and he could not be sure.

But Hades had given his word; he had to believe—and so he visualized the girl behind him, following him as he led. And he walked steadily, through the Field of Asphodel toward the gates of Tartarus. The gates opened as he approached. Cerberus was still asleep in the middle of the road. He stepped over him. Surely he could hear her now, walking behind him. But he could not turn around to see, and he could not be sure because of the cry of vultures which hung in the air above the river Styx like gulls over a bay. Then, on the gangplank, he heard a footfall behind him, surely. . . . Why, oh why, did she walk so lightly? Something he had always loved, but he wished her heavier-footed now.

He went to the bow of the boat and gazed sternly ahead, clenching his teeth, and tensing his neck until it became a thick halter of muscle so that he could not turn his head. On the other side, climbing toward the passage of Avernus, the air was full of the roaring of the great cataracts that fell chasm-deep toward Styx, and he could not hear her walking and he could not hear her breathing. But he kept a picture of her in his mind, walking behind him, her face growing more and more vivid with excitement as she approached the upper air. Then finally he saw a blade of light cutting the gloom, and knew that it was the sun falling through the narrow crevasse which is Avernus, and that he had brought Eurydice back to earth.

But had he? How did he know she was there? How did he know that this was not all a trick of Hades? Who calls the gods to judgment? Who can accuse them if they lie? Would Hades, implacable Hades, who had had the great Asclepius murdered for pulling a patient back from death, would that powerful thwarting mind that had imagined the terrain of Tartarus and the bolts of those gates and dreamed a three-headed dog—could such a mind be turned to mercy by a few notes of music, a few tears? Would he who made the water shrink always from the thirst of Tantalus and who toyed with Sisyphus' stone, rolling it always back and forth—could this will, this black ever-curdling rage, this dire fancy, relent and let a girl return to her husband just because the husband had asked? Had it been she following him through the Field of Asphodel, through the paths of Tartarus, through the gates, over the river? Had it been she or the echoes of his own fancy—that cheating mourner's fancy, which, kind but to be cruel, conjures up the beloved face and voice only to scatter them like smoke? Was it this, then? Was this the final cruelty? Was this the torment Hades had promised? Was this the final ironic flourish of death's scepter, which had always liked to cudgel poets? Had he come back without her? Was it all for nothing? Or was she there? Was she there?

Swiftly he turned, and looked back. She was there. It was she. He reached his hand to take her and draw her out into the light—but the hand turned to smoke. The arm turned to smoke. The body became mist, a spout of mist. And the face melted. The last to go was the mouth with its smile of welcome. Then it melted. The bright vapor blew away in the fresh current of air that blew through the crevasse from the upper world.

Narcissus and Echo

Of all the nymphs of river and wood, a dryad named Echo was the best beloved. She was not only very beautiful and very kind, but had a haunting musical voice. The other dryads and naiads and creatures of the wood begged her to sing to them and tell them stories—and she did. She was a great favorite of Aphrodite, who used to come all the way from Olympus to chat with Echo and listen to her tales. Being goddess of love, she was especially concerned with gossip—which is mostly about who loves whom and what they are doing about it. And Echo kept her entertained as no one else could.

Aphrodite said, "All the world asks me for favors, Echo. But not you. Tell me, is there not someone you would wish to love you? Some man, boy, god? Just name him, and I will send my son Eros, who will shoot him with his arrow and make him fall madly in love with you."

But Echo laughed and said, "Alas, sweet Aphrodite, I have seen no man who pleases me. And gods are too fickle. Man and boy—I look at them all very carefully—but none seems beautiful enough to match my secret dream. When the time comes, I shall ask your help—if it ever comes."

"Well, you are lovely enough to demand the best," said Aphrodite. "On the other hand, the best happens only once. And who can wait so long? However, I am always at your service."

Now Echo did not know this, but at that moment the most beautiful boy in the whole world was lost in that very wood, trying to find his way out. His name was

84

Narcissus, and he was so handsome that he had never been able to speak to any woman except his mother. For any girl who saw him immediately fainted. Of course this also gave him a very high opinion of himself. And as he went through the woods, he thought:

"Oh, how I wish I could find someone as beautiful as I. I will not be friends with anyone less perfect in face or form. Why should I? This leaves me lonely, true, but it's better than lowering myself."

So he walked along the path, but he was going the wrong way, getting more and more lost. In the other part of the wood Echo had just said farewell to Aphrodite, and was coming back to the hollow tree in which she lived. She came to a glade in the forest and there saw something that made her stop in astonishment and hide behind a tree. For whom did she see but Zeus himself—king of the gods, lord of the sky. He was leaning on his volt-blue lightning shaft, holding a river nymph by the shoulder, and she was smiling up at him.

"Well," said Echo. "He's at it again. Won't Aphrodite enjoy hearing about *this!*"

But then her attention was caught by something else. She turned to see a tall purple-clad figure moving through the trees toward the glade. She recognized Hera, queen of the gods, jealous wife of Zeus, and she realized that Hera must have heard of what Zeus was doing, and was coming to catch him. And so the kind-hearted nymph hurried forward and curtsied low before Hera, saying, "Greetings, great queen. Welcome to the wood."

"Hush, fool!" whispered Hera. "Don't say a word! I am trying to take someone by surprise."

"This is a proud day for us," said Echo, thinking swiftly, "to be visited by so many gods. Just two minutes ago, Zeus was here looking for you."

"Zeus? Looking for *me?* Are you sure?"

"The great Zeus. Your husband. He asked me whether I had seen you. Said he had heard you were coming this way, and he wished very much to meet you. When I told him I had not seen you, he flew off looking very disappointed."

"Really? Can it be so? Zeus looking for me? Disappointed? Well—miracles never cease. Which way did he go?"

"Oh—toward Olympus."

"Thank you, child," said Hera. "I'll be going too."

And she disappeared.

In the meantime Zeus, hearing voices, had hidden himself and the river nymph in the underbrush. When Hera left, he came out, and to thank Echo he gave her a shining blue sapphire ring from his own finger.

Hera, having returned to Olympus, found that Zeus was not there. She realized that something was wrong and sped back to the forest. The first thing she saw was Echo admiring a large sapphire ring that burned on her finger like a fallen star. Hera recognized the ring and immediately understood that the nymph had tricked her in some way and had been given the ring as a reward.

"Wretched creature!" she cried. "I know what you have done. I see the gift you have been given. And I would not have it said that my husband is more generous than I. So I too shall reward you for what you have done. Because you have used your voice for lying, you shall never be able to say anything to anyone again— except the last words that have been said to you. Now try lying."

"Try lying," said Echo.

"No more shall you meddle in high concerns—no more shall you gossip and tell stories and sing songs— but endure this punishment evermore . . ."

"Evermore . . ." said Echo, sobbing.

And Hera went away to search for Zeus. And the nymph, weeping, rushed toward her home in the hollow tree. As she was going she saw once again the dazzling brightness that was the face of a god and she stopped to see. It was no god, but a lad about her own age, with yellow hair and eyes the color of the sapphire Zeus had given her. When she saw him, all the grief of her punishment dissolved and she was full of a great laughing joy. For here was the boy she had been looking for all her life, as beautiful as her secret dream—a boy she could love.

She danced toward him. He stopped and said, "Pardon me, but can you show me the path out of the wood?"

"Out of the wood . . ." said Echo.

"Yes," he said. "I'm lost. I've been wandering here for hours, and I can't seem to find my way out of the wood."

"Out of the wood . . ."

"Yes. I've told you twice. I'm lost. Can you help me find the way?"

"The way . . ."

"Are you deaf, perhaps? Why must I repeat everything?"

"Repeat everything . . ."

"No, I will not! It's a bore! I won't do it!"

"Do it . . ."

"Look, I can't stand here arguing with you. If you don't want to show me the way, well then, I'll just try to find someone who can."

"Who can . . ."

Narcissus glared at her and started away. But she came to him and put her arms around him and tried to kiss his face.

"Oh, no—none of that!" said Narcissus, shoving her away. "You're just like all the rest of them, aren't you? They faint, and you say stupid things. Stop it! You can't kiss me."

"Kiss me . . ."

"No!"

"No . . ."

And she tried to kiss him again. Again he pushed her aside. She fell on her knees on the path and hugged his legs and lifted her lovely tear-streaked face to his, trying to speak. But she could not.

"No!" he said. "Let go! You can't hold me here. I will not love you."

"Love you . . ."

He tore himself from her grip and strode away. "Farewell," he called.

"Farewell . . ."

She looked after him until he disappeared. And when he was gone, she felt such sadness, such terrible tearing grief, such pain in every part of her, that it seemed she was being torn apart by white-hot little pincers, torn flesh from bone. And since she could not speak, she said this prayer to herself:

"Oh, Aphrodite, fair goddess, you promised me a favor. Do me one now. Hear me though I am voiceless. My love has disappeared, and I must disappear too, for I cannot bear the pain."

And Aphrodite, in the garden on Olympus, heard this prayer—for prayers do not have to be spoken to be heard. She looked down upon the grieving nymph and pitied her and made her disappear. Her body melted into thin cool air, so that the pain was gone. All was gone . . . except her voice, for Aphrodite could not bear to lose the sound of that lovely story-telling voice. The goddess said, "I grant you your wish—and one thing more. You have not asked vengeance upon the love that has betrayed you. You are too sweet and kind. But *I* shall take vengeance, nevertheless. I decree now that whoever has caused you this pain will know the same terrible longing. He will fall in love with someone who cannot return his love—and will forever desire and never achieve."

But Narcissus knew nothing of this—of Echo's grief nor Aphrodite's vow. He wandered the forest path, thinking, "All these girls who love me on sight—it's too bad I cannot find one as beautiful as I. For until I do, I shall not love. And all their loving will be only vexation to me."

He sat down on the bank of a river to rest. Not a river really, but a finger of the river—a clear little stream moving slowly through rocks. The sun shone on it; it became a mirror, holding the trees and the sky upside down, and a small silver trembling sun. And Narcissus, looking into the stream, saw a face.

He blinked his eyes and looked again. It was still there—the most beautiful face he had ever seen. As beautiful, he knew, as his own, but with a nimbus of light behind it so that the hair was blurred and looked long—like a girl's. He gazed and gazed and could not have enough of it. He knew that he could look upon this face forever and still not be satisfied. He put out his hand to touch her. The water trembled and she disappeared.

"A water nymph," he thought. "A lovely dryad—daughter of the river god, no doubt. The loveliest of his daughters. She is shy. Like me, she can't bear to be touched. Ah—here she is again."

The face looked at him out of the stream. Again, very timidly, he reached his hand. Again the water trembled and the face disappeared.

"I will stay here until she loves me," he said to himself. "She may hide now, but presently she will recognize me too. And come out." And he said aloud: "Come out, lovely one."

And the voice of Echo, who had followed him to the stream, said, "Lovely one . . ."

"Hear that, hear that!" cried Narcissus, overjoyed. "She cares for me too. You do, don't you? You love me."

"Love me . . ."

"I do—I do—Finally I have found someone to love. Come out, come out—Oh, will you never come out?"

"Never come out . . ." said Echo.

"Don't say that, please don't say that. Because I will stay here till you do. This, I vow."

"I vow . . ."

"Your voice is as beautiful as your face. And I will stay here, adoring you forever."

"Forever . . ."

And Narcissus stayed there, leaning over the stream, watching the face in the water, watching, watching . . . sometimes pleading with it to come out, hearing its voice answer. Coaxing, begging, looking. . . . Day after day he stayed there, night after night, never moving, never eating, never looking away from the face. He stayed there so long that his legs grew into the bank of the river and became roots. His hair grew long, tangled, leafy. And his pale face and yellow hair became delicate yellow and white petals—the flower Narcissus, which lives on the riverbank and leans over watching its reflection in the water.

And there you can find it till this day. And in the woods too, when all is still, you will sometimes come upon Echo. And if you call to her in a certain way, she will answer your call.

Eros and Psyche

There was a king who had three daughters, and the youngest, named Psyche, was so beautiful that Aphrodite grew jealous and began to plan mischief.

"I'll teach that little upstart," she said to herself. "How dare she go around pretending to be as beautiful as I? When I get through with her, she'll wish she'd been born ugly as a toad."

She called her son Eros to her and said, "Son, your

mother has been insulted. See that castle down there? In a bower there, a maiden lies asleep. You must go pierce her with one of your arrows."

"While she is asleep? What good will it do?"

"No good at all. Just evil, which is exactly what I plan for her."

"But she can fall in love only with the one she is looking at when the arrow pierces her. Why bother when she is asleep?"

"Because if you scratch her with the arrow while she sleeps, she will form a passion for the first one she sees when she awakes. And I will take care to supply her with someone very special—the castle dwarf, perhaps. Or the gardener, who has just celebrated his hundred-and-second birthday. Or a donkey—yes that's possible too. I haven't decided. But you can be sure it will be someone quite undesirable. Her family will be surprised."

"This is a cruel trick, Mother."

"Oh, yes—it's meant to be cruel. I tell you the girl has irritated me. Now be off and do your work."

Obediently, Eros flew down to the castle. He made himself invisible and flew through the window into the girl's chamber. He stood looking at her.

"She is very beautiful," he thought. "Too beautiful for her own safety, poor girl."

He leaned over her, holding his dart so as to delicately scratch her shoulder. But he must have made some sound, for she opened her eyes then and looked straight into his, although she could not see him. And her huge black brilliant eyes startled him, so that the dart slipped and he scratched his own hand. He stood there feeling the sweet poison spread in his veins, confused, growing dizzy with joy and strangeness. He had spread love, but never felt it; shot others, but never been wounded himself. And he did not know himself this way.

The girl closed her eyes and went to sleep again. He stood looking at her. Suddenly she had become the most wonderful, the most curious, the most valuable thing in the world to him. And he knew that he would never let her come to any harm if he could prevent it. He thrust his dart into his quiver and flew back to Olympus.

When he told his mother what had happened, she fell into a rage and ordered him out of her sight. She then flung a curse upon Psyche. She cast an invisible hedge of thorns about her, so that no suitor could come near. The beautiful young princess became very lonely and very sad. Her father and mother could not understand why no one offered to marry her.

Now the gods often quarrel, but Olympus had never seen such a feud as now flared between Aphrodite and her son.

"How dare you torment the girl like that?" he said to his mother. "So long as you keep this spell upon her, I will do no business of love. I will shoot no one with my arrows. Your praises will not be sung. And without praise you will dry up and become a vicious old harpy. Farewell."

And indeed Eros refused to shoot his arrows. People stopped falling in love with one another. There was no praise for Aphrodite; her temples stood empty, her altars unadorned. No marriages were made, no babies born. The world seemed to grow old and dull in a day. Without love, work died. Farmers did not plough their fields. Ships crawled listlessly on the seas. Fishermen scarcely cast their nets. Indeed, there were not many fish to catch, for they had sunk sullenly to the very bottom of the sea. And Aphrodite herself, goddess of love and beauty, found herself wasting in the great parching despair that came off the earth like a desert wind.

She called her son to her and said, "I see that you must have your way. What is it you wish?"

"The girl," he said.

"You shall have her. Sharpen your darts now and get back to work, or we shall all run melancholy mad."

So Eros filled his quiver with arrows, stood upon a low cloud, and shot as fast as he could. And man and woman awakened to each other again. Fish leaped in the sea. Stallions trumpeted in the fields. Sounds of the earth holding revel came to the goddess on the mountain, and she smiled.

But the parents of Psyche still grieved. For now with all the world celebrating the return of love, and the most unlikely people getting married, still no one asked for their daughter. They went to the oracle, who said:

"Psyche is not meant for mortal man. She is to be the bride of him who lives on the mountain and vanquishes both man and god. Take her to the mountain and say farewell."

As the king and queen understood this, they thought that their daughter was intended for some monster, who would devour her as so many other princesses had been devoured to appease the mysterious forces of evil. They dressed her in bridal garments and hung her with jewels and led her to the mountain. The whole court followed, mourning, as though it were a funeral instead of a wedding.

Psyche herself did not weep. She had a strange dreaming look on her face. She seemed scarcely to know what was going on. She said no word of fear, wept no tear, but kissed her mother and father goodbye, and waited on the mountain, standing tall, her white bridal gown blowing about her, her arms full of flowers. The wedding party returned to the castle. The last sound of their voices faded. She stood there listening to a great silence. The wind blew hard, hard. Her hair came loose. The gown whipped about her like a flag. She felt a great pressure upon her and she did not understand. Then a huge breathy murmur, the wind itself howling in her ear, seemed to say, "Fear not. I am Zephyrus, the west wind, the groom's messenger. I have come to take you home."

She listened to the soft howling and believed the words she seemed to hear and was not afraid, even though she felt herself being lifted off the mountain, felt herself sailing through the air like a leaf. She saw her own castle pass beneath her and thought, "If they're looking up and see me now, they'll think that I'm a gull." And she was glad that they would not know her.

Past low hills, over a large bay, beyond forests and fields and another ring of hills, the wind took her. And now she felt herself coasting down steeps of air, through the failing light, through purple clumps of dusk, toward another castle, gleaming like silver on a hilltop. Gently, gently, she was set down within the courtyard. It was empty. There were no sentries, no dogs, nothing but shadows, and the moon-pale stones of the castle. She saw no one. But the great doors opened. A carpet unreeled itself and rolled out to her feet. She walked over the carpet, through the doors. They closed behind her.

A torch burned in the air and floated in front of her. She followed it. It led her through a great hallway into a room. The torch whirled. Three more torches whirled in to join it, then stuck themselves in the wall and burned there, lighting the room. It was a smaller room, beautifully furnished. She stepped onto the terrace which looked out over the valley toward the moonlit sea.

A table floated into the room and set itself down solidly on its three legs. A chair placed itself at the table. Invisible hands began to set the table with dishes of gold and goblets of crystal shells. Food appeared on the plates, and the goblets filled with purple wine.

"Why can I not see you?" she cried to the invisible servants.

A courteous voice said, "It is so ordered."

"And my husband? Where is he?"

"Journeying far. Coming near. I must say no more."

She was very hungry after her windy ride. She ate the food and drank the wine. The torch then led her out of the room to another room that was an indoor pool, full of fragrant warm water. She bathed herself. Fleecy towels were offered her, a jeweled comb, and a flask of perfumed oil. She anointed herself, went back to her room, and awaited her husband.

Presently she heard a voice in the room. A powerful voice speaking very softly, so softly that the words were like her own thoughts.

"You are Psyche. I am your husband. You are the most beautiful girl in all the world, beautiful enough to make the goddess of love herself grow jealous."

She could not see anyone. She felt the tone of the voice press hummingly upon her, as if she were in the center of a huge bell.

"Where are you?"

"Here."

She reached out her arms. She felt mighty shoulders, hard as marble, but warm with life. She felt herself being enfolded by great muscular arms. And a voice spoke: "Welcome home."

A swoon of happiness darkened her mind. The torches went out, one by one.

When she awoke next morning, she was alone. But she was so happy she didn't care. She went dancing from room to room, exploring the castle, singing as she went. She sang so happily that the great pile of stone was filled with the sound of joy. She explored the castle, the courtyard, and the woods nearby. One living creature she found, a silvery greyhound, dainty as a squirrel and fierce as a panther. She knew it was hers. He went exploring the woods with her and showed her how he could outrace the deer. She laughed with joy to see him run.

At the end of the day she returned to the castle. Her meal was served by the same invisible servants. She again bathed and anointed herself. At midnight again her husband spoke to her, and she embraced him and wondered how it was that of all the girls in the world she had been chosen for this terrible joy.

Day after day went by like this, and night after night. And each night he asked her, "Are you happy, little one? Can I bring you anything, give you anything?"

"Nothing, husband, nothing. Only yourself."

"That you have."

"But I want to see you. I want to see the beauty I hold in my arms."

"That will be, but not yet. It is not yet time."

"Whatever you say, dear heart. But then, can you not stay with me by day as well, invisible or not. Why must you visit me only at night?"

"That too will change, perhaps. But not yet. It is too soon."

"But the day grows so long without you. I wait for nightfall so, it seems it will never come."

"You are lonely. You want company. Would you like your sisters to visit you?"

"My sisters—I have almost forgotten them. How strange."

"Do you care to renew your acquaintance?"

"Well, perhaps. But I don't really care. It is you I want. I want to see you. I want you here by day as well as by night."

"You may expect your sisters here tomorrow."

The next day the west wind bore Psyche's elder sisters to the castle and landed them in the courtyard, windblown and bewildered. Fearful at having been snatched away from their own gardens, they were relieved to find themselves deposited so gently in the courtyard. How much more amazed they were, then, to see their own sister, whom they thought long dead, running out of the castle. She was more beautiful than ever, blooming with happiness, more richly garbed than any queen. She stormed joyously out of the castle, swept them into her arms, embraced and kissed them, and made them greatly welcome.

Then she led them into the castle. The invisible servants bathed and anointed them and served them a sumptuous meal. And with every new wonder they saw, with every treasure their sister showed them, they grew more and more jealous. They too had married kings, but little local ones, and this castle made theirs look like dog kennels. They did not eat off golden plates and drink out of jewels. Their servants were the plain old visible kind. And they ate and drank with huge appetites and grew more and more displeased with every bite.

"But where is your husband?" said the eldest one. "Why is he not here to welcome us? Perhaps he didn't want us to come."

"Oh, he did, he did," cried Psyche. "It was his idea. He sent his servant, the west wind, for you."

"Oho," sniffed the second sister. "It is he we have to thank for being taken by force and hurled through the air. Pretty rough transport."

"But so swift," said Psyche. "Do you not like riding the wind? I love it."

"Yes, you seem to have changed considerably," said the eldest. "But that's still not telling us where your husband is. It is odd that he should not wish to meet us—very odd."

"Not odd at all," said Psyche. "He—he is rarely here by day. He—has things to do."

"What sort of things?"

"Oh, you know—wars, peace treaties, hunting—you know the things that men do."

"He is often away then?"

"Oh, no! No—that is—only by day. At night he returns."

"Ah, then we will meet him tonight. At dinner, perhaps—"

"No—well—he will not be here. I mean—he will, but you will not see him."

"Just what I thought!" cried the eldest. "Too proud to meet us. My dear, I think we had better go home."

"Yes, indeed," said the second sister. "If your husband is too high and mighty to give us a glimpse of his august self, then we're plainly not wanted here."

"Oh, no," said Psyche. "Please listen. You don't understand."

"We certainly do not."

And poor Psyche, unable to bear her sisters' barbed hints, told them how things were. The two sisters sat at the table, listening. They were so fascinated they even forgot to eat, which was unusual for them.

"Oh, my heavens!" cried the eldest. "It's worse than I thought."

"Much much worse," said the second. "The oracle was right. You *have* married a monster."

"Oh, no, no!" cried Psyche. "Not a monster! But the most beautiful creature in the world!"

"Beautiful creatures like to be seen," said the eldest. "It is the nature of beauty to be seen. Only ugliness hides itself away. You have married a monster."

"A monster," said the second. "Yes, a monster—a dragon—some scaly creature with many heads, perhaps, that devours young maidens once they are fattened. No wonder he feeds you so well."

"Yes," said the eldest. "The better you feed, the better he will later."

"Poor child—how can we save her?"

"We cannot save her. He's too powerful, this monster. She must save herself."

"I won't listen to another word!" cried Psyche, leaping up. "You are wicked evil-minded shrews, both of you! I'm ashamed of you. Ashamed of myself for listening to you. I never want to see you again. Never!"

She struck a gong. The table was snatched away. A window flew open, and the west wind swept in, curled his arm about the two sisters, swept them out and back to their own homes. Psyche was left alone, frightened, bitterly unhappy, longing for her husband. But there were still many hours till nightfall. All that long hideous afternoon she brooded about what her sisters had said. The words stuck in her mind like poison thorns. They festered in her head, throwing her into a fever of doubt.

She knew her husband was good. She knew he was beautiful. But still—why would he not let her see him? What did he do during the day? Other words of her sisters came back to her:

"How do you know what he does when he's not here? Perhaps he has dozens of castles scattered about the countryside, a princess in each one. Perhaps he visits them all."

And then jealousy, more terrible than fear, began to gnaw at her. She was not really afraid that he was a monster. Nor was she at all afraid of being devoured. If he did not love her she wanted to die anyway, but the idea that he might have other brides, other castles, clawed at her and sent her almost mad. She felt that if she could only see him her doubts would be resolved.

As dusk began to fill the room, she took a lamp, trimmed the wick, and poured in the oil. Then she lighted it and put it in a niche of the wall where its light could not be seen. She sat down and awaited her husband.

Late that night, when he had fallen asleep, she crept away and took the torch. She tiptoed back to where he slept and held the lamp over him. There in the dim wavering light she saw a god sleeping. Eros himself, the archer of love, youngest and most beautiful of the gods. He wore a quiver of silver darts even as he slept. Her heart sang at the sight of his beauty. She leaned over to kiss his face, still holding the lamp, and a drop of hot oil fell on his bare shoulder.

He started up and seized the lamp and doused its light. She reached for him, felt him push her away. She heard his voice saying, "Wretched girl—you are not ready to accept love. Yes, I am love itself and I cannot live where I am not believed. Farewell, Psyche."

The voice was gone. She rushed into the courtyard, calling after him, calling, "Husband! Husband!" She heard a dry cracking sound, and when she looked back, the castle was gone too. The courtyard was gone. Everything was gone. She stood among weeds and brambles. All the good things that had belonged to her vanished with her love.

From that night on she roamed the woods, searching. And some say she still searches the woods and the dark places. Some say that Aphrodite turned her into an owl, who sees best in the dark and cries, "Who . . . ? Who . . . ?"

Others say she was turned into a bat that haunts old ruins and sees only by night.

Others say her husband forgave her, finally; that he came back for her and took her up to Olympus, where she helps him with his work of making young love. It is her special task, they say, to undo the talk of the bride's family and the groom's. When mother or sister visit bride or groom and say, "This, this, this . . . that, that, that . . . better look for yourself; seeing's believing, seeing's believing," then she calls the west wind, who whips them away, and she, herself, invisible, whispers to them that none but love knows the secret of love, that believing is seeing.

Arion

Wise men of science have now decided that certain animals may be able to speak, and have begun to question dolphins to find out if this is true.

The old stories are full of clever beasts. Talking is the least they did. The dolphin, in particular, frisks through the blue waters of mythology. There is something about this playful fish which has always tickled the fancy of those who tell stories. So the scientists are in good company.

There is the story of Arion. He was the son of Poseidon and a naiad, and favored by Apollo, who taught him to play the lyre most beautifully. Arion lived in Corinth. He was a brave adventurous young man, and wanted very much to travel. But an oracle had said, "No ship will bring you back from any voyage you make."

So he was forced to stay at home. For his twentieth birthday Apollo gave him a golden lyre, and he was wild to try it out at music festivals held in Sicily and Italy.

"Oracles are gloomy by nature," he said to himself. "It is rare you hear of a happy prophecy. Besides, I must see the world no matter what happens."

Thereupon he took his lyre and set sail for Italy. He competed in the festival at Tarentum and won all the prizes. He played and sang so beautifully that the audience was mad with delight and heaped gifts upon him: a jeweled sword, a suit of silver armor, an ivory bow and a quiver of bronze-tipped arrows. He was so happy and triumphant that he forgot all about the prophecy, and took the first ship back to Corinth, although the captain was a huge, ugly, dangerous-looking fellow, with an even uglier crew.

On the first afternoon out, Arion was sitting in the bow, gazing at the purple sea and absently fingering his lyre, when the captain strode up and said, "Pity . . . you're young to die."

"Am I to die young?" said Arion.

"Yes."

"How do you know?"

"Because I'm going to kill you."

"That does seem a pity," said Arion. "When is this sad event to take place?"

"Soon—in fact, immediately."

"But why? What have I done?"

"Something foolish. Permitted yourself to become the owner of a treasure which I must have. That jeweled sword, that silver armor—you should never show things like that to thieves."

"Why don't you take what you want without killing me?"

"No. We thought it over and decided it would be better to kill you. It usually is in these cases. Then the person who's been robbed can't complain, you see. Makes it safer for us."

"Well, I see you've thought the matter over carefully," said Arion. "So I have nothing more to say. One favor, though: Let me sing a last song before I die."

At the music festival Arion had invented a song of praise, called the dithyramb. He sang one now—praising first Apollo, who had taught him music, and then his father, Poseidon, master of the sea. Then he sang a song of praise to the sea itself and all who dwell there—the naiads and Nereids and gliding fishes. He sang to the magical changefulness of these waters, which put on different colors as the sun climbs and sinks, silver and amethyst in the early light, hot blue at noon, smoky purple at dusk. He sang to the sea, smiling, treacherously kind, offering the gift of cool death for any hot grief.

So singing, he leaped from the bow of the vessel, lyre in hand, and plunged into the sea.

He had sung so beautifully that the creatures of the deep had risen to hear him. His most eager listeners were a school of dolphins, who love music. The largest dolphin dived under him and rose to the surface lifting Arion on his back.

"Thank you, friend," said Arion.

"A poor favor to return for such heavenly music," said the dolphin.

The dolphin swam away with Arion on his back, the other dolphins frisking about, dancing on the water, as Arion played. They swam very swiftly, and Arion arrived at Taenarus and made his way to Corinth a day before the ship was due. He went immediately to the palace, to his friend, Periander, King of Corinth, and told him his story. Then he took the king down to the water front to introduce him to the dolphin. The king ordered his smith to make a gold saddle for the dolphin, and invited it to stay in the castle moat whenever it was in the neighborhood.

The next day the ship arrived in port. Captain and crew were seized by the king's guard and taken to the castle. Arion stayed hidden.

"Why have you taken us captive, O King?" said the captain. "We are peaceable law-abiding sailors."

"My friend Arion took passage on your ship!" roared the king. "Where is he? What have you done with him?"

"Poor lad," said the captain. "He was quite mad. He was on deck singing to himself one day, and then suddenly jumped overboard. We put out a small boat, circled the spot for hours. We couldn't find a trace. Sharks, probably. The sea's full of them there."

"And what do you sailors do to a man-eating shark when you catch him?" asked the king.

"Kill him, of course," said the captain. "Can't let them swim free and endanger other sailors."

"A noble sentiment," said Arion, stepping out of his hiding place. "And that's exactly what we do to two-legged sharks in Corinth."

So captain and crew were taken out and hanged. The ship was searched, and Arion's property restored to him. He insisted on dividing the rich gifts with the king. When Periander protested, Arion laughed and said, "Treasures are trouble. You're a king and can handle them. But I am a minstrel. I must travel light."

And all his life he sang songs of praise. His music grew in power and beauty until people said he was a second Orpheus. When he died, Apollo set him in the sky, him and his lyre and the dolphin too. And they shine in the night sky still, the stars of the constellation Arion. They shine on pirates and minstrels, on wise men trying to learn the language of animals, and on simple men who have always known it.

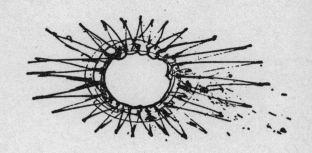

DEMIGODS

Perseus

King Acrisius of Argos was uncertain in battle, unlucky in the hunt, and of fitful, flaring temper. He sat brooding in his throne-room.

"My daughter, Danae, grows tall and ripe," he said to himself. "Her eyes fog over when I speak to her. She is ready for a husband, but am I ready for a son-in-law? I dislike the idea and always have. A son-in-law will be a younger man waiting for me to die so he can take the throne. Perhaps he will even try to hasten that sad event. Such things are not unknown. I loathe the idea of a son-in-law. But she is ready for a husband, and princesses must not be spinsters . . . a grave decision . . . I shall consult the oracle."

THE PROPHECY

He sent to the oracle at Delphi, and the messenger returned with this prophecy: "Your daughter will bear a son who will one day kill you."

Acrisius had the messenger beheaded for bringing bad news and retired to his throne-room to continue his brooding.

"The auguries of the Pythoness are supposed to be immutable." he said to himself. "But are they? How can they be? What if I were to slay my daughter now while she is still childless; how then could she have a son to kill me? But, must I kill her to keep her childless? Is it not sufficient to forbid her male company all her days? Would I not be accomplishing the same purpose without calling upon my head the vengeance of the gods? Yes, that is a much better plan."

Thereupon he shut the beautiful young girl in a brass tower which he had specially built with no doors and only one window, a slit too narrow for a child to put an arm through. The tower was surrounded by a high spiked wall patrolled by armed sentries and savage dogs. Here Acrisius locked his daughter away, and so murderous was his temper in those days that no one dared asked him what had become of the laughing young girl.

Acrisius stayed away from the tower and waited for someone to bring him word that his daughter had died;

but the news he was waiting for did not come, and he wondered what was keeping her alive. How could a girl like that, a princess used to hunting, swimming, and running free on the hillsides, a girl who had never had her wishes crossed in her life—how could she stand this imprisonment?

He rode past the brass tower which glittered in the hot sunlight. The brass helmets of the sentries glittered as did the brass collars on the necks of the huge dogs. As he rode past, he tried to see through the slit, tried to glimpse her face looking out, but the brass glitter was so bright he could not see.

The king took to watching the tower from his own castle wall, but the tower was far away, across a valley on the slope of a hill. The tower was only a splinter of light, but it seemed to glow more and more hotly until it hurt his eyes. One night he could not sleep so he went out on his castle wall in the night wind and looked out across the valley. It was a black night—no moon, no stars. The hill was only a thicker darkness. Then, suddenly, as if a torch were lighted, the tower burned clear, shining as brightly as if it were day instead of night; but the tower was lit from the inside now—the brass walls flaring more whitely, like silver, casting a dim radiance over the valley and throwing the giant shadow of trees past the hill.

Amazed and fearful, Acrisius summoned his soldiers, leaped on his horse, and rode to the tower. As they galloped toward it, the light died, and the burning tower subsided into the hillside. He led his soldiers up to the black wall. The dogs were howling. The sentries recognized the king and opened the gate. He galloped through and rode up to the slit window. Then, through the snarling of the sounds and the clatter of weapons, he heard another sound, sudden as an arrow—the sound of a baby crying.

The brass tower had no doors, having been built with no doors, so now Acrisius bade his soldiers take sledges and batter the brass walls. When the wall was breached the king stepped through and entered his daughter's cell. There in the torchlight he saw her sitting on a bench nursing a baby. She looked up at him and, smiling secretly, said, "I have named him Avenger." The word for avenger in Greek is *Perseus*.

The king's first thought was to kill mother and child, but he had a second thought. "She must be under special protection; of Apollo himself, perhaps, master of the Delphic Oracle, who does not wish his prophecies thwarted. I can die but once, true enough; but if she is being protected by the gods, and I kill her, then they will torture me through eternity. Well, we shall test the quality of her protectors."

Acrisius ordered that Danae and the baby be taken from the prison and put in a wooden boat without sails, without oars, and without food or water. "Yes," he said to himself, "we shall test the drift of events. If she is under divine patronage, the ship will be guided safely to harbor. If, on the other hand, it runs into misfortune, then, obviously, she is not being protected by the gods, and the accident of her death will bring upon me no high reprisal. Yes, I like this idea."

Thereupon, the princess and her infant son were set adrift in an empty skiff without sails and without oars. Acrisius returned to his castle and went to sleep.

Danae sat up straight in the boat and tasted the night wind as it sang past her face and whipped her hair about her shoulders. The baby laughed for joy and reached his hands to catch the glittering points of the waves. All night they drifted, and the next day, and the next night. A light rain fell, giving them water to drink; and a gull dropped a fish right into the boat, giving them food. On the second morning Danae saw that they had drifted into the lee of an island. Fishing boats stood off the shore, and fishermen were casting their nets.

She shouted. One of the slender boats sailed toward them. The fishermen was a huge, bearded fellow named Dictys who took them on board and put into shore. He was amazed by the beauty of the girl and by the impudence of the baby who pulled boldly at his beard and gurgled, but did not cry.

Dictys took mother and child to King Polydectes of the island of Sephiros. Polydectes too was amazed at the beauty of the young woman. He called her daughter and offered her the hospitality of the island—a house to live in and servants to wait upon her—and paid Dictys the value of a month's catch for the prize he had drawn from the sea.

THE ISLAND

Perseus grew to be a strong, fearless lad. He loved to run, to swim, to hunt, to fight with the other boys. At night, lying near the fire, he loved to hear his mother tell stories that made his brain flame with excitement— stories of the gods, of heroes, of monsters, of battles, of transformations, and of strange loves.

She told him about the three sisters called the Gorgons who were very tall and beautiful with long golden hair and golden wings. She told of how the youngest and most beautiful, named Medusa, flew into one of Athene's temples to meet with Poseidon, risen secretly from the sea. Athene, learning of this, became enraged and wove a spell upon her loom; and Poseidon, below, awakened to find that he was holding a monster in his arms. Medusa's eyes bulged as if someone were strangling her, and a swollen blackened tongue forced her mouth open, showing the yellow fangs of her teeth. Her fingers and toes were brass claws; and, worst of all, each golden hair was now a live, hissing snake. Poseidon roared with fury, cast her aside, and dived into the sea. Medusa spread her wings and flew away, weeping, to find her sisters. She was so horrible to look upon that everyone who saw her face was turned to stone. So her sisters took her to a far place, a secret place, where they lived together plotting revenge upon Athene.

Perseus made his mother tell this story over and over again for, like many children, he was fond of stories that frightened him. Best of all, though, he liked to hear of the days when his mother had been shut up in the brass tower: how she had been so sad she thought she must die; how she would look out of the slit in the wall and see nothing but a single star; how she gazed at that star, magnified by her tears, until it seemed to fill the whole sky. Its light fell keen as a sword-blade through the blackness; and, as she watched, the blade of light flashed through the slit in the brass wall filling the dark chamber with a golden light. The gold pulsed, thickened, and gathered itself into a tall column of light and formed itself into the shape of a man, but such a man as she had never seen . . . taller than mortal man with golden hair and hot golden eyes, wearing gold bracelets on his mighty arm, and carrying a volt-blue zigzag shaft of pure light as other men carry spears.

She knelt before him. She knew he was a god, but he raised her up and said, "Yes, I am a god, but do not be afraid. I come as a man."

"He rode the golden light every night into my dungeon," she said to Perseus, "and was always gone by dawn . . . as the morning star vanishes when day begins."

"And was he my father?" asked Perseus.

"He was your father. And some day he will return to me, I know. That is why I must not take another husband, for how can I love an ordinary man, remembering him?"

"So I am the son of a god?" said Perseus.

"Yes."

"What does that make me?"

"A hero. Or a very great scoundrel." She smiled and drew the boy to her. "But let us hope that you too will rescue maidens and thwart mad kings. Sometimes, as now, with the firelight in your eyes, you look quite like him, but not so tall, not so tall."

So Perseus grew to manhood. He was the most splendid young man on all the island. He could outrace, outswim, outclimb, outfight any other lad on Sephiros; but he raged at the peacefulness of the times because he wished to try himself in battle.

Now there was one who had watched Perseus grow with great displeasure. King Polydectes, long in love with the beautiful Danae, was very eager to get rid of her fierce, young son so that he might compel her to marry him. He was a sly one, Polydectes, sly and patient and very cruel in his quiet way, and he made a skillful plan to rid himself of Perseus. He spread the news he was to marry a princess of another island and invited all the young men of Sephiros to the palace. There he asked them, as was the custom, for gifts which he would bring to the bride.

"What she loves above all else is a fine horse," he told the young men. "And I have promised her fifty splendid stallions. Will each of you select the best of his herd?"

All the young nobles promised, except Perseus, for he had nothing of his own, living as he did on the bounty of the king.

"Well, Perseus," said Polydectes. "I hear nothing but

silence from you. What gift will you bring? What do you offer your king and your host who has been so generous with you and your dear mother over the years?"

Polydectes had studied Perseus well and felt sure that the boy's flaming pride would lead to some rash offer—that was the whole point of his pretended marriage and the gathering at the palace.

"I do not wish to embarrass you, Perseus," he said. "I know that you do not have the resources of these other young men; but surely I can expect a token gift, a rabbit you might snare, perhaps, or a fish you might catch."

"Oh, King," cried Perseus. "Oh, Host and Benefactor, I owe you too much gratitude to repay you with the common gift of a horse. I shall bring you the head of Medusa!"

The throne-room rang with laughter, but Polydectes' face was grave. "You choose to jest," he said. "That is not courteous for a guest of such long standing."

"I do not jest," cried Perseus. "Promises are sacred to me. I will bring you the head of Medusa, or you can take my own. This is a pact of blood, Polydectes."

Perseus turned and strode out of the throne-room. He went to a cliff overlooking the sea and, stretching his arms to the sky, said, "Oh, unknown father on Olympus—Zeus, or Apollo, or Ares, or whoever you may be who visited my mother in a shower of gold— grant your son one boon. Not the head of Medusa. I shall win that for myself, but I need to know where she is and how to get there. Please help me."

He dropped his arms and stared at the blank sky, which seemed more blue and more empty than ever before.

"Good day, brother," he heard a voice say.

He whirled around. There stood a magnificent creature with a round hat, a laughing face, a jaunty beard, winged sandles, and a golden staff entwined with serpents. Perseus knew that it was the god, Hermes, and that he should fall on his knees; but his knees would not bend, so he bowed instead.

"Our father, Zeus, is away on one of his trips," said Hermes, "but in his absence I do some of his business so I am here to serve you. What is all this now about the head of Medusa?"

Perseus told him of the rash promise he had made to Polydectes.

"Rash, indeed," murmured Hermes. "Foolhardy, in fact. It's a family trait, I suppose. God-seed and human make a strange mixture, a ferment in the blood; leads to great exploits or great folly. But . . . folly itself can be the seed of exploit. Let us see what we can do."

"I need . . ."

"Please, allow me to tell you what you need. First of all, I must tell you that sister Athene takes a special interest in your case. She is responsible for Medusa's petrifying aspect, you know, and is a sworn enemy of the Gorgon sisters. She sends you these."

Hermes reached into his pouch and pulled out a pair of Talaria, silver-winged sandals like those he himself wore. "She is not only a potent spinster," he said, "but she cobbles magically too. She made me my winged shoes, and now she has made you a pair. With these you can fly more swiftly than an eagle. Now, listen, and I will tell you what to do. Set out today. Fly north. Search until you find the Gray Sisters. When you find them you must force them to tell where you can find the Nymphs of the West; no one else can tell you. These Nymphs have in their keeping certain pieces of equipment which you will need to kill Medusa. Without these implements you must fail . . . Come down, Perseus! How can I speak to you when you're up there? Come down. You can practice later."

Perseus laughed with joy, turned a somersault in the air, then hovered above Hermes' head, ankle-wings whirring like the wings of a humming bird.

"I heard you," he cried. "I heard you. Gray Sisters, Nymphs of the West . . . their secrets will be my weapons. Thank you, dear brother. Thank you, Hermes. Thank Athene for me. Farewell."

He turned so that the setting sun was on his left hand and sped away, shouting, "I can fly! I can fly!"

THE QUEST

Gulls screamed, amazed, at the tall thing which flew but did not fish; falcons stooped for a closer look, then flew away; and Perseus flashed over the sea to where the land began again—a fair, rich land. He flew over fields of wheat and groves of olive trees, herds of sheep and cows, tiny villages and white cities. The land became wilder, and mountains stood up with only a few poor villages clinging to their sides. Behind the first mountains were taller crags topped with snow, the first snow Perseus had ever seen. He flew past these mountains, great forests, a plain full of rivers, and another range of mountains where neither man nor beast was to be seen. A hailstorm raged, spitting hard sharp pieces of ice at Perseus so that he had to wrap his face in his cloak as he flew.

When the storm blew itself out, Perseus found himself over the sea again, a sea of ice, not flat but full of great billows and troughs as if it had frozen all at once during a gale. The sun was a huge pale moon peering heavily over the edge of the sky. The air was so cold he could hardly breathe.

Perseus heard a thin cackling, keener than the wind. He dipped and saw three hunched figures. Thereupon, he raised his arms, pointed his toes, and plunged to earth feet-first, landing among the three Gray Sisters. Three hags they were, very long and lean. They had been born old countless years before time began and had grown older every day since. They had gray hair, never cut, so long it fell to the ground and dragged behind them as they walked. Their skin was gray; they wore no clothes, just their long gray hair; and their skin was tough and wrinkled as an alligator's. Their bare feet were like leather claws.

They sat in a close circle, scolding and jabbering and tittering. They kept snatching at each other's hands, and then Perseus saw that they had but a single eye and a single tooth for the three of them. They quarreled constantly, snatching the eye and tooth away from each other.

"Give me the eye!" cried one. "I want to see! My turn to see!"

"Give me the tooth—then you will see me, see me . . . you will see me smiling."

"I want the tooth for biting. If you take the tooth, then I must have the eye."

"And what will *I* have—I, I, I? . . ."

Swiftly Perseus stepped among them, shuddering as his hand touched their withered claws. Swiftly he seized the tooth and eye and stepped back.

"Where's the tooth? Give me the tooth!"

"Where's the eye? Give me the eye!"

"It's my turn! You've had it too long!"

"My turn . . . my turn."

"I don't have it."

"I don't have it."

"I don't have it."

"Where is it? . . . Where's the tooth? . . . Where is it,

where's the eye? . . . You have it . . . You must have
it . . . No, you, you, you—"

"I have it," said Perseus. "I have them both, tooth
and eye."

"A stranger!"

"A thief!"

"A *man!*"

"A man! Give me the eye so that I may see him!"

"A man! Give me the tooth so that I may smile at
him!"

"But *he* has them."

"Oh, yes, he has them."

"Give them back to us, young sir, so that we may see
you and smile at you . . . Please . . . please . . ."

"I have your tooth and your eye," said Perseus, "and
I will return them to you only in exchange for your secret."

"What secret? What secret?"

"Where do I find the Nymphs of the West?"

"Oh, that secret. No, we may not tell. No, it's a secret within a secret, and they are for keeping, not for
telling. We dare not tell. It's a Gorgon secret; they will
rip us to pieces if we tell."

"You belong to the Immortals and cannot die," said
Perseus, "so you will crouch here through the ages with
no tooth in your mouth, no eye for your head. And
while you may do without smiling or without chewing,
you will soon be wanting your eye. Oh, yes . . . think
how long and dark the moments are for two of you
when the third sister has the eye. Think of your darkness now. Think of the torment of hearing a voice and
not being able to see who is speaking, and it has only
been a few minutes. Think then of these minutes
stretching into hours, and the hours into days, and the
days into months, and the months into years—dark
years, endless, boring, heavy, dark years with mind and
memory growing emptier and emptier . . ."

"Give us the eye, the eye! Keep the tooth, and give us the eye!"

"There is a little jelly in my hand. It lies between my thumb and forefinger. Just a bit of pressure, a bit more, and it will be crushed, useless, unable to see. I am impatient. I must have the secret. I must know where to find the Nymphs of the West. The secret! Quickly! My finger is pressing my thumb. The jelly trembles. Can you not feel the pain in your empty sockets?"

"Aieeee . . ."

"Stop!"

"Do not crush it! We will tell . . . We will tell . . ."

"Quickly then."

And, speaking together swiftly, sobbing and tittering and sighing, they told him how to find the Nymphs of the West, who alone could give him what he needed to overcome Medusa.

Now who were these nymphs, and why were they the guardians of this secret? . . . Ages past, when Hera married Zeus, Mother Earth gave her as a wedding present a tree that bore golden apples. Hera loved this tree very much, but after a while she found she could not keep it in her own garden for Zeus would steal the beautiful golden apples and distribute them as favors to the nymph or dryad or naiad or Titaness or human girl he happened to be courting at the time. Therefore, Hera took her magic tree and planted it at the very end of the earth, on the uttermost western isle, a place of meadows and orchards of which Zeus knew nothing. Here it was that the Titan, Atlas, stood, shoulders bowed, forehead knotted, legs braced, holding up the end of the sky. It was the three daughters of Atlas, enchantingly beautiful nymphs, whom Hera appointed to guard the treasure. It was a wise decision. These lush and fragrant dryads made better guards than any dragon or three-headed dog or sea-serpent for such monsters could be killed or chained or outwitted, but no one could get past the nymphs. They danced among the trees and shouted gay invitations to the marauder until he forgot all about his quest and came to dance with them. Then they would stroke him and give him wine to drink and dance him about in circles until he was so befuddled they could do what they chose with him. Then they would dance him to the edge of the cliff and push him into the sea. They did all this under the eye of their father, Atlas, who groaned occasionally under his burden, or stamped his foot, making the earth shake, or shrugged his shoulders, making comets fall. These strange storms of the Titan's grief gave the island a bad name; fishermen avoided it, and sailors. Other dark secrets came to be buried here with the Nymphs of the West, and they guarded them with the same fatal skill with which they guarded the golden apples. So it was that they held the Gorgon secret.

Now, following the directions of the Gray Ones, Perseus flew west. He flew and flew over a strange misty sea until he saw the mighty hunched figure of Atlas holding up the sky. Then he dipped toward earth. The nymphs were dancing when a shadow flew over the grove.

"It's Hermes!"

"Welcome, sweet Herald! Welcome, dear cousin!"

"Come down! . . . Come quickly! Tell us all the news!"

Perseus came lower and hovered a few feet above the ground.

"*He's* not Hermes!"

"But he has Hermes' sandals. Hermes has a helper! Oh joy!"

"Not a god at all, a man! A lovely young one. All fresh and clean and lovely."

"Come down, man!"

"Come play with us, stay with us . . ."

"Come dance with us."

"You must be a great thief to steal Hermes' sandals; come tell us how you did it."

"Come down . . . Come down . . ."

Still standing on air, Perseus bowed. "Nothing would give me greater pleasure than to dance with you and tell you stories, but I have a promise to keep first, a promise to keep, weapons to get, an enemy to kill."

"Oh, you foolish men with your ridiculous quests, your oaths and enemies and impossible voyages. When will you learn to eat the fruit and spit out the pits and sleep without dreaming in the arms of your beloved? Have you ever slept in a woman's arms, sweet young sir?"

"My mother's."

"Your mother's . . . Good for a start, but not enough, not enough. Come kiss us, lad—we need kissing. It has been a dry summer."

"I cannot kiss you now," said Perseus. "Even up here I smell your apple-blossom scent, and grow bewildered, and almost forget who I am. What then if I were to come close and touch your apple-ruddy skin and drink your cider breath? I would grow drunk as bees among honey suckle, lose my sting, and forget my oath. Please help me, Nymphs. Do not bewilder me."

"Come down . . . stop this talking, and come down . . . Forget your quest, we'll give you something better. Come down . . ."

"Look, you lovelies," said Perseus. "My father was Zeus who wooed my mother as a shaft of fire, a fountain of light. My birth was strange, and the auguries thereof. Deeds are my destiny, adventure my profession, and fighting my pleasure. Unless I fight and win, I am no good for love either. Have you ever seen a rooster after he is beaten in a fight? His comb sags, he is unfit for love, he disappoints his hens. Tell me your secret. Give me what I need to fight Medusa. Tell me where to find her, and I will go there. By the gods, I will come back with her head in my pouch. Then, then, then I will be fit for you, beautiful ones. I will come back and tell you the tale of my battle, and other tales too, and dance with you, and do your pleasure."

"He speaks well, sisters. He must be the son of a god."

"He is our cousin then. We owe him loyalty."

"The Gorgons are our cousins too."

"But so ugly. So ugly and so foul. I prefer this handsome new cousin."

"Yes, I like this one, this flyer with his bright yodel and silver spurs. He will keep his promise, I know. He will come back and tread his chicks most nobly."

"Let us tell him . . . quickly . . . the sooner we tell, the sooner he will go, and the sooner he will return."

"I smell rain on the wind. With any luck the clouds will come and hide the eyes of Father Atlas so he cannot see us dance with the stranger and grow jealous."

"Quickly, then . . ."

They ran to Perseus and, seizing his ankles, pulled him down, and clung to him, kissing and whispering. He grew dizzy with their apple fragrance and the touch of their smooth hands and the taste of their lips; but they were not trying to befuddle him now, only to touch him because they were unable to reveal anything to anyone they could not touch. And when he put their whisperings and murmurings together he learned what he had to know about where the Gorgons dwelt and how to find Medusa.

Then they pulled him to a huge tree whose twisted roots stood half out of the ground. They searched among these roots and gave him three things: a shield of polished bronze, bright as a mirror, and he was told that he must never look at Medusa herself but only at her reflection in the shield; a sword, sickle-shaped, slender and bright as the new moon; and, lastly, a Cap of Darkness—when he put it on he disappeared altogether, and they had to grope about to catch him and to extract three kisses each for the three gifts.

He took off his Cap of Darkness and rose a bit in the air, gleaming with happiness. "Thank you, sweet Nymphs. Thank you, beautiful cousins. With these gifts I cannot fail."

"Will you keep your promise? . . . Will you come back and tell us your story? . . . Will you come back to dance and play? Will you come back another day? . . ."

"Farewell . . . Farewell . . ." cried Perseus. He rose to the top of the trees, smiled at the sight of Hera's golden apples shining among the leaves, and resolved to steal one when he came back to take home to his mother. Then he soared away past Atlas' angry face, scowling back at him; he flashed past the mighty shoulder of the Titan and flew northward again, following the outer rim of the earth.

With the Cap of Darkness on his head, invisible as the wind, Perseus followed the curve of the dark sea that girdles the earth until he came to the Land Beyond—the Land of the Hyperboreans where the sea is a choked marsh, and the sky is low and brown, and the weeds give off a foul stench. Here, he had been told, was where the Gorgons dwelt.

He came to earth, picked his way through the rattling weeds, and came to a kind of stone orchard which looked like one of our own graveyards, a grove of statues. Looking closer, he saw that they were the old, worn-down stone figures of men and beasts; and he realized that he was looking at those who had seen Medusa's face and had been turned to stone between one breath and the next. There was a stone child running, a stone man dismounting from a stone horse, and stone lovers, touching. Perseus closed his eyes and took a deep breath. He drew his new-moon sword, held it ready, and raised his bright shield. He had to judge all his movements by the weight of things because the Cap of Darkness made him invisible even to himself.

Now, going silently as he could, he made his way among the terrible stone figures until he heard a sound of snoring. He stood still and looked. Glittering in the muddy light were brass wings. He raised his shield now, not daring to look directly, and held it as a mirror and guided himself by the reflection. In a covering of weeds lay three immensely long, bulky shapes. He saw brass wings and brass claws. Two of them slept as birds sleep with their heads tucked under their wings. But the third one slept with her face uncovered. Perseus saw the hair of her head stand up and writhe as he looked into his mirror shield, and he knew that it was Medusa. He felt the roots of his own hair prickling with horror as if they too were turning into snakes.

He kept the shield in front of his face and walked backward. The head of Medusa grew larger in the shield. He saw the snakes swelling, writhing furiously, darting their tongues, biting each other in their fury at the stranger's approach so that their blood ran like sweat over her forehead. He tilted his shield to keep her head in the center because she was directly below him now. He smelled the terrible stench of the bleeding snakes. Then he raised his sword, and, guiding himself by the reflection, struck a savage downward backhand blow, feeling the horror, anger, pride, and pleasure of battle mingling in him like a mighty potion, firing him with the furious triumph of the deed done at the very moment of the doing. His sword whipped with a magical momentum, shearing its way through the snakes, through the thick muscles and tendons, through the lizard toughness of her hide, through bone and gristle and sinew, striking off the monster head as a boy whips off the head of a dandelion in the field.

Swiftly he stooped, scooped up the head by its limp dead snakes, stuffed it into his pouch, and stood amazed for where her blood had fallen, two creatures sprang up, a warrior holding a golden sword and a beautiful white horse with golden mane and golden hooves and astounding golden wings. They were Chrysaor and Pegasus, children of Poseidon, whom Medusa had been unable to bear while she lived as a monster, and who had grown full-size in her womb.

But Perseus did not stop to look as the sisters were waking. He sprang into the air and flew off as fast as he could. The Gorgons, without losing an instant, spread their brass wings and climbed into the air and sped after him, howling. He wore the Cap of Darkness, and they could not see him; but they could smell the blood of the cut-off head and followed the spoor like hounds of the air, howling. He did not dare look back but heard the clatter of their brass wings and the snapping of their great jaws. Athene, however, had cobbled well, magically well. His sandals carried him faster than the Gorgons could fly. He drew away from them until he heard only a very faint tinkle and a cry like wind-bells chiming. Then he lost them altogether.

THE RETURN

Perseus had his prize. Medusa's head was wet and fresh in his pouch, and he was eager to get back to Sephiros to boast to his mother and make Polydectes eat his words; but first he had promises to keep.

Therefore, he flew back to the Island of the

Hesperides and danced with the three Apple Nymphs. All night they danced in the orchard. They danced him as they had never danced a marauder before. They whirled him among the trees, one after the other, then all together, faster and faster. He grew drunk as a bee on their apple fragrance, their ruddy skin, and their petal touch. He was a hero! He had just finished his first quest; killed his first enemy. He was drunk on triumph too, strong with joy. He danced and strutted and gleamed. When dawn came he saluted it with a great bawling golden-voiced challenge. He celebrated like a hero, and the nymphs were so giddy with pleasure that they watched him helping himself to a golden apple from Hera's tree and only smiled.

But now the ground trembled. The sky growled thunderously. It was full morning now. The mist that had been hiding the eyes of Atlas had blown away, and the Titan looked down and saw his daughters enjoying themselves in the orchard, a sight he could not endure. He stamped his foot and made the earth shake, roared thunderously, and shrugged his shoulders making comets fall, huge flaming bolts of rock that bombarded the orchard, setting fire to the apple trees.

Perseus' blood rose as murder sang in his heart. He flew straight toward Atlas' mighty face, poised there before the gargantuan frown, and, standing on air, opened his pouch and drew out Medusa's head. The Titan turned to stone. He was a mountain now, holding up the western end of the sky. It is a mountain till this day— Mt. Atlas.

"Farewell!" shouted Perseus. "Farewell, sweet cousins . . . beautiful nymphs. Farewell, my apple-lovelies."

"Will you come again? Will you come again? . . ."

"Will I not?" cried Perseus. "Every mid-summer I will return, and we will do the orchard dance again until the trees flame. Farewell . . ." and he flew away.

Southward he flew, then eastward. He crossed a desert; and now, far below, he saw the first gleam of that matchless blue that belonged to his own sea. But as he followed the Philistine shoreline which is the eastern boundary of that sea, he saw a very strange sight: a naked girl chained to a rock and, pushing toward that rock, the huge blunt head of a sea monster. The shore was black with people, an ant-swarm of people, watching.

He came lower and saw that the girl was wearing magnificent jewels. She was not weeping, but gazing straight ahead, blankly. On the shore, in front of the crowd, stood a tall man and woman wearing crowns. Perseus took a quick look and saw that the monster was still some way off. He dropped to earth and, taking off his Cap of Darkness, spoke to the man wearing the crown, "Who are you? Who is the girl, and what is the sacrifice? Is it a private ceremony or one decreed by the gods? My name is Perseus, and I wish to know."

The Queen put her face in her hands, and wept. The King said, "I am Cepheus, king of Joppa. This is my wife, Cassiopeia, and that unfortunate girl is my daughter, Andromeda. My wife, foolish, boastful woman was vain of her beauty and that of our daughter—not without reason, as you see; but she took it into her head to praise herself among the people, saying that she and Andromeda were more beautiful than any Nereid, who, as you may know, are very jealous and enjoy the patronage of Poseidon. So they went weeping to the god of the sea, saying my wife had insulted them and demanding vengeance. Poseidon sent that sea serpent, longer than a fleet of warships, whose breath is fire, to harry our coast, destroy our shipping, burn our villages, and devour our cattle. I consulted the oracle who told me that the only way I could wipe out my wife's offense was to sacrifice my daughter to the monster. I love my daughter; but I am king, and private woe must yield to public welfare. Therefore you see her, the lovely innocent child, bound to the rock, and the beast swims near, swims near . . ."

Perseus said, "When public welfare battens on private woe, there is a great disorder in events, a filthy confusion that needs the cleanliness of a sword. Poseidon is my uncle, King, and I feel free to play with his pets."

Perseus heard the water hiss, saw spouts of steam rise as the monster's scorching breath ruffled the surface and made the sea boil. He knew they had spoken too long. Without waiting to put on his Cap of Darkness, he drew his sword and leaped into the air. Over the beast's head he flashed and fell like lightning, right onto the great scaly back. He rode the monster there, in the water, hacking at the huge head with his new-moon sword until the flames of the beast's breath were laced with blood, and the great neck split like a log under the woodman's ax.

The monster sank. Perseus flew off his back, dripping wet, flew to the rock, struck away Andromeda's chains, lifted her in his arms, and bore her gently through the air to where her mother and father stood.

"Here is your daughter," said Perseus, "but only briefly, very briefly, for I claim her as my bride."

"As your bride?" shouted Cepheus. "What do you mean? Do you think I shall give my daughter, Andromeda, the most richly dowered princess in the East, to an unknown vagabond?"

"I may be a vagabond," said Perseus, "but I shall not long be unknown. If you were not going to be my father-in-law, Cepheus, I should explain to you what kind of fool you are. For the sake of family harmony, however, I forbear. You were content to serve your daughter up as dead meat to this monster as the price of your wife's vanity because he came well-recommended, but you refuse to give her, warm and alive, to him who slew the monster. And why? Simply because it is unexpected. Father-in-law or not, you are a fool, Cepheus, a pitiful fool; and if by word or deed you seek to prevent me from taking your daughter, you will be a dead fool. I do not ask your leave, I am announcing my intention. Say goodbye to your parents, Andromeda." Perseus lifted her in his arms again and flew away.

When he landed on Sephiros, he was amazed to find the island deserted. His mother was not at home, nor was anyone in the village. He hurried to the castle and found it blazing with light. There was a clamor of shouting and laughter and a clatter of weapons. He forced his way through a crowd of revellers, and entered the throne-room.

There he saw his mother, deathly pale, but loaded with jewels, sumptuously garbed, her beautiful bare white arm in the swarthy clutch of Polydectes. Now Perseus understood that the king had taken advantage of his absence to force Danae to marry him. He had returned just in time.

His great voice clove the uproar. "Polydectes—ho!"

All voices ceased. The king stood rigid, staring at him, his face fixed in an amazed snarl. Perseus saw him gesture to his guards. They drew their swords and stepped forward, twenty of them.

"I have brought you your gift, Polydectes," said Perseus. "Your wedding gift. Remember? Different bride, same gift."

He put his hand into his pouch. "Mother!" he shouted. "Close your eyes!"

He drew out the head of Medusa, and the throne-room became a grove of statues. Stone guards stood with stone swords upraised. One held a javelin, about to plunge it into Perseus' back. A statue of Polydectes, mouth frozen in a scream. Among all the frozen shapes of terror and wrath, the white beloved trembling figure of his mother, Danae.

He put the head in his pouch, stepped to Danae, and took her in his arms. "Be happy, mother," he said. "I am home now. Your danger is a dream, your enemy has become his own monument."

"It is the gods," she whispered. "Their whim is implacable; their caprice, our fate. Look, Perseus . . ." She led him to one of the stone figures. A bearded old man wearing a crown.

"Who is that?"

"Your grandfather, Acrisius, one of the guests, attending the nuptials of a fellow-king. He did not know that I was the bride."

"Your father? He who shut you in the tower?"

"Shut me there to thwart the prophecy . . . that his grandson would kill him."

"Delighted to oblige," said Perseus. "I never did fancy his style. Shut you up in a dungeon . . . Met another parent like that recently. Oh, that reminds me. Come home. I want you to meet your daughter . . ."

It was Perseus' own wedding night; but before he received his bride, he went to the temple of Athene and the temple of Hermes to thank them for what they had done. He made them gifts: he gave the bright shield to Athene, a very curious shield now, permanently emblazoned with the reflection of Medusa's head which had burned itself on the metal; the Cap of Darkness to Hermes. He very much wanted cap and shield for himself, but he knew that gods who give gifts expect a rich return. However, he did keep the winged sandals and the new-moon sword. He knew that his deeds had just begun and that he would have a great deal of traveling and fighting to do in days to come.

As for Medusa's head, it was too dangerous to keep. He threw it into the sea. It sank to the bottom, where it still rests, pushed here and there by the tides, passing islands, making coral where it goes.

Daedalus

The gods, being all-powerful, needed a more subtle praise than obedience. They preferred their intention to become man's aspiration, their caprice, his law. Athene, in particular, liked to be served this way. The gray-eyed goddess of wisdom, whose sign was the owl, taught men the arts they needed to know, not through gross decree, but through firing the brightest spirits to a white heat wherein they perceived the secret laws of nature and made discoveries and inventions.

Now, in those times, her favorite among all mortals was an Athenian named Daedalus. In the white city of the goddess Daedalus was honored among all men, and treasure after treasure flowed from his workshop—the wheel, the plough, the loom. Finally, as happens to many men, his pride raced away with his wits; and he fell into a black envy of his own nephew, Talos, a most gifted lad, whom he had taken into his workshop, and who, everyone said, was bound to follow in his footsteps.

"Aye, but he's following too fast," grumbled Daedalus to himself. "He's treading on my heels."

Daedalus, at that time, was working on a special project, a blade to cut wood more quickly than knife or ax. He had puzzled, tested, and tried many things, but nothing seemed to work. Then, one day, coming early to his workshop, he heard a curious sound. It was his nephew, Talos, who had come even earlier. He was leaning over, holding a board pinned to a low table under his knee, and swiftly cutting into it with what looked like the backbone of a fish.

The boy turned to him, smiling. "Look, uncle," he cried. "See, how splendid! Yesterday I saw a large fish stranded on the beach, half-eaten by gulls, and a notion came to me that his spine with its many sharp teeth might be just the thing we're looking for. So I took it from the fish who had no more need of it and tried it right there. I cut through a great piece of driftwood. Isn't it wonderful? Don't you think the goddess, Athene, herself, washed the fish on shore for me to see? Why are you looking at me that way, uncle? Are you not pleased?"

"Very pleased, my boy. I have long been considering your case and have been weighing how to reward you according to your merit. Well, now I think I know. But first we must go to Athene's temple to give thanks for this timely inspiration."

He took the boy by the hand and led him up the sunny road to the top of the hill, to the Acropolis where the temple of Athene stood—and still stands. Daedalus led him to the roof of the marble building; and there, as the lad stretched his arms toward heaven, Daedalus stepped softly behind him, placed his hands on his shoulders, and pushed. The boy went tumbling off the temple, off the hill, to the rocks below. But Athene who had heard the first words of the boy's prayer, caught him in mid-air, and turned him into a partridge, which flew away, drumming. She then withdrew her favor from Daedalus.

Word of the boy's death flashed through the city. Nothing could be proved against Daedalus, but he was the target of the darkest suspicions, which, curiously enough, he took as an affront, for nothing could be proved, and so he felt unjustly accused.

"Ungrateful wretches!" he cried. "I will leave this city. I will go elsewhere and find more appreciative neighbors."

He had not told them about his invention of the saw, but took the model Talos had made and set out for Crete. Arriving there, he went directly to the palace of King Minos, who, at that time, was the most powerful king in all the world, and made him a gift of the marvelous tool that could cut wood more swiftly than knife or ax. Minos, delighted, immediately appointed Daedalus Court Artificer, Smith Extraordinary, and fitted out a workshop for him with the likeliest lads for apprentices. Minos also gave the old fellow a beautiful young slave girl for his own.

Now, the Cretan women were the loveliest in the world, and Crete's court the most glittering. The capital city of Knossos made Athens seem like a little village. Women and girls alike wore topless dresses, gems in their hair, and a most beguiling scent made by slaves who had been blinded so that their noses would grow more keen. Daedalus was an honored figure at this court—and a novelty besides. The Cretans were mad for novelties so the old man was much flattered and content.

He was a special favorite with the young princesses, Ariadne and Phaedra, who loved to visit him at his workshop and watch him make things. He became very fond of the girls and made them marvelous jointed wooden dolls with springs cunningly set and coiled so that they curtsied and danced and winked their eyes. Queen Pasiphae also came to see him often. He made her a perfume flask that played music when it was uncorked and a looking glass that allowed her to see the back of her head. She spent hours with him gossiping for she was very bored.

The queen kept coaxing Daedalus to tell her why he had really left Athens for she sensed a secret; but all he would ever say was that the goddess, Athene, had withdrawn her favor, so he had been forced to leave her city.

"Goddess Athene!" she cried. "Goddess this and god that . . . What nonsense! These are old wives' tales, nursery vapors, nothing for intelligent men and women to trouble themselves about."

"Oh, my lady," cried Daedalus. "In heaven's name, take care what you say. The gods will hear, and you will be punished."

"And I took you for a sophisticated man," said the queen. "A man of the world, a traveler, a scientist. I am disappointed in you. Gods, indeed! And are you not, my smith, more clever by far than that lame Hephaestus? And am I not more beautiful than Aphrodite?"

She stood up tall and full-bodied, and, indeed, very beautiful. The old man trembled.

"Come here. Come closer. Look at me. Confess that I am more beautiful than the Cytherean . . . Aphrodite. Of all the gods, she is the one I disbelieve in most.

Love . . . my serving maids prate of it, my daughters frisk with the idea. All through the island men meet women by rock and tree, their shadows mingle; and I, I have Minos, the crown on a stick who loves nothing but his own decrees."

"Softly, madame, softly," said Daedalus. "You are not yourself. It is midsummer, a confusing time for women; what they say then must be discounted. Your wild words will be forgiven, but please do not repeat them. Now, see what I have made for you, even as you were saying those foolish things: a parasol, lighter than a butterfly's wing, and yet so constructed that it opens by itself like a flower when it feels the sun."

But Aphrodite had heard, and she planned a terrible vengeance.

Now, Minos had always been very fond of bulls, especially white ones. He was not aware that this was a matter of heredity, that his mother, Europa, had been courted by Zeus who had assumed the guise of a white bull for the occasion. The king knew only that he liked white bulls. And, since he was in a position to indulge his preferences, he sent through all the world for the largest, the finest, and the whitest. Finally, one arrived, the most splendid bull he had ever seen. It was dazzling white, with hot black eyes, polished hooves, and coral-pink nostrils; its long sharp horns seemed to be made of jet. The king was delighted and sent for all the court to see his fine new bull.

He had no way of knowing that the animal had been sent there by Aphrodite, and neither did Pasiphae. As soon as the queen saw the bull, she felt herself strangling with a great rush of passion. She fell violently, monstrously, in love with the bull. She came to Daedalus and told him.

"What shall I do?" she moaned. "What can I do? I'm going mad. It's tearing me to pieces. You are the cleverest man in the world. Only you can help me. Please, please, tell me what to do."

Daedalus could not resist the beautiful queen; besides she had touched his vanity. He had to prove himself clever enough to help her in her impossible wish. He thought and thought, and finally went to work. He fashioned a wooden cow with amber eyes, real ivory horns, and ivory hooves and tenderly upholstered it with the most pliant cowhide. It was hollow, and so shaped that Pasiphae could hide herself inside. He put wheels on the hooves, and springs in the wheels. That night, as the moon was rising, the great white bull saw the form of a graceful cow gliding toward him over the meadow, mooing musically.

The next morning, Pasiphae came to the workshop. She gave Daedalus a great leather bag full of gold, and said, "Be careful, old friend. This secret is a deadly one."

Both Pasiphae and Daedalus were good at keeping secrets; but this was one that had to come out for, after a while, the queen gave birth to a child, who attracted a great deal of notice as he was half bull. People derisively called him the Minotaur, or Minos' bull.

Even in his most cruel fury. Minos was a careful planner. He decided to hide his shame, knowing that the world forgets what it does not see. He had Daedalus construct a tangled maze on the palace grounds, a place of thorny hedges and sudden rooms called the Labyrinth. There were paths running this way and that, becoming corridors, plunging underground, crossing each other, crossing themselves, each one leading back to the middle, so there was no way out.

Here King Minos imprisoned Pasiphae and the

Minotaur—and Daedalus too. Minos wanted to make
very sure that the old craftsman would never divulge
the secret of the Labyrinth so here Daedalus dwelt. His
workshop was in the Labyrinth, but he did not work
well. At his bench he could hear Pasiphae howling, and
the hideous broken bellowing of the bull-man, who
grew more loathsome and ferocious each day.

His only comfort was his son, Icarus, who, of his
own free will, chose to live with him because he so
loved and admired his father. It was Icarus who said to
him one day, "Father, I grow weary of this maze. Let us
leave this place and go to places I have not seen."

"Alas, dear boy," said Daedalus, "we cannot. It is
forbidden to leave the Labyrinth."

"You know the way out, do you not? You built the
thing, after all."

"Yes, certainly, I know the way out. But I dare not
take it. Minos would have us put to death immediately.
All I can do is petition the king to allow you to go, but I
must remain."

"No. We go together."

"But I have explained to you that we cannot."

"Minos is a great king," said Icarus. "But he does
not rule the whole earth. Let us leave the island. Let us
leave Crete and cross the sea."

"You are mad, dear boy. How can we do this? The
sea is locked against us. Every boatman on every craft,
large and small, is under strict interdict against allowing
me voyage. We cannot leave the island."

"Oh, yes, we can," said Icarus. "I'll tell you how.
Just make us wings."

"Wings?"

"To fly with. Like the birds—you know—wings."

"Is it possible? Can I do this?"

"Birds have them; therefore, they have been made.
And anything, dear father, that has been made you can

duplicate. You have made things never seen before, never known before, never dreamed before."

"I will start immediately," cried Daedalus.

He had Icarus set out baits of fish and capture a gull. Then, very carefully, he copied its wings—not only the shape of them, but the hollow bone struts, and the feathers with their wind-catching overlaps and hollow stems, and he improved a bit on the model. Finally, one day, he completed two magnificent sets of wings with real feathers plucked from the feather cloaks the Cretan dancers used. They were huge, larger than eagles' wings.

He fitted a pair to Icarus, sealing the pinions to the boy's powerful shoulders with wax. Then he donned his own.

"Goodbye to Crete!" cried Icarus joyfully.

"Hear me, boy," said Daedalus. "Follow me closely and do not go off the way. Do not fly too low or the spray will wet your wings, not too high or the sun will melt them. Not too high and not too low, but close by me, through the middle air."

"Oh come, come," cried Icarus, and he leaped into the air, spreading his wings and soaring off above the hedges of the Labyrinth as if he had been born with wings. Daedalus flew after him.

They flew together over the palace grounds, over the beaches, and headed out to sea. A shepherd looked up and saw them; and a fisherman looked up and saw them; and they both thought they saw gods flying. The shepherd prayed to Hermes, and the fisherman prayed to Poseidon, with glad hearts. Now, they knew, their prayers would be answered.

Icarus had never been so happy. In one leap his life had changed. Instead of groveling in the dank tunnels of the Labyrinth, he was flying, flying free under the wide bright sky in a great drench of sunlight, the first boy in the history of the world to fly. He looked up and saw a gull, and tried to hold his wings steady and float on the air as the gull was doing, as easily as a duck floats on water. He felt himself slipping, and he slipped all the way in a slanting dive to the dancing surface of the water before he could regain his balance. The water splashing his chest felt deliciously cool.

"No . . . no . . . ," he heard his father call from far above. "Not too low and not too high. Keep to the middle air . . ."

Icarus yelled back a wordless shout of joy, beat his wings, and soared up, up, toward the floating gull.

"Ha . . . ," he thought to himself. "Those things have been flying all their lives. Wait till I get a little practice. I'll outfly them all."

Crete was a brown dot behind them now; there was no land before them, just the diamond-glittering water. Old Daedalus was beating his way through the air, steadily and cautiously, trying this wing-position and that, this body angle and that, observing how the gulls thrust and soared. He kept an eye on Icarus, making mental notes about how to improve the wings once they had landed. He felt a bit tired. The sun was heavy on his shoulders. The figures spun in his head.

"I must not go to sleep," he said to himself. "I must watch the boy. He may do something rash."

But Icarus was flying easily alongside so Daedalus hunched his shoulders, let his chin fall on his chest, and half-coasted on a column of air. He shut his eyes for a moment . . . just for a moment . . .

In that moment Icarus saw a great white swan climb past him, wings spread, shooting like a great white arrow straight for the sun and uttering a long honking call. Icarus looked after him; he had already dwindled and was a splinter of light, moving toward the sun.

"How splendid he is, flying so swiftly, so proudly,

so high. How I should like to get a closer look at the sun. Once and for all I should like to see for myself what it really is. Is it a great burning eye looking through an enormous spyhole, as some Libyans say; or is it Apollo driving a golden coach drawn by golden horses, as the Athenians believe; or perhaps is it a great flaming squid swimming the waters of the sky, as the barbarians say; or, maybe, as my father holds, is it a monster ball of burning gas which Apollo moves by its own motion. I think I shall go a bit closer, anyway. The old man seems to be napping. I can be up and back before he opens his eyes. How splendid if I could get a really good look at the sun and be able to tell my father something he doesn't know. How that would delight him. What a joke we will have together. Yes . . . I must follow that swan."

So Icarus, full of strength and joy, blood flaming in his veins, stretched his home-made wings and climbed after the swan. Up, up, up, he flew. The air seemed thinner, his body heavier; the sun was swollen now, filling the whole sky, blazing down at him. He couldn't see any more than he had before; he was dazed with light.

"Closer . . ." he thought. "Higher . . . closer . . . up and up . . ."

He felt the back of his shoulders growing wet.

"Yes," he thought. "This is hot work."

But the wetness was not what he supposed; it was wax—melting wax. The wax bonds of his wings were melting in the heat of the sun. He felt the wings sliding away from him. As they fell away and drifted slowly down, he gazed at them, stupefied. It was as if a great golden hand had taken him in its grasp and hurled him toward the sea. The sky tilted. His breath was torn from his chest. The diamond-hard sea was rushing toward him.

"No," he cried. "No . . . no . . ."

Daedalus, dozing and floating on his column of air, felt the cry ripping through his body like an arrow. He opened his eyes to see the white body of his son hurtling down. It fell into the sea and disappeared.

Theseus

Young Theseus had a secret. He lived with his mother in a little hut on a wild sea-battered part of the coast called Troezen. For all his poor house and worn-out clothes, he was very proud, for he had a secret: he knew that he was the son of a king. His mother had told him the story one night when their day's catch of fish had been very bad and they were hungry.

"A king, truly," she said. "And one day you will know his name."

"But mother, then why are you not a queen and I a prince? Why don't we live in a palace instead of a hovel?"

"Politics, my son," she said sadly. "All politics . . . You're too young to understand, but your father has a cousin, a very powerful lord with fifty sons. They are waiting for your father to die so they can divide the kingdom. If they knew he had a son of his own to inherit it, they would kill the son immediately."

"When can I go to him? When can I go there and help my father?"

"When you're grown. When you know how to fight your enemies."

This was Theseus' secret . . . and he needed a secret to keep him warm in those long, cold, hard years. One of his worst troubles was his size. His being small for his age bothered him terribly for how could he become a great fighter and help his father against terrible enemies if he couldn't even hold his own against the village boys? He exercised constantly by running up and down the cliffs, swimming in the roughest seas, lifting logs and rocks, bending young trees; and indeed he grew much stronger, but he was still very dissatisfied with himself.

A VOICE FROM THE SEA

One day, when he had been beaten in a fight with a larger boy, he felt so gloomy that he went down to the beach and lay on the sand watching the waves, hoping that a big one would come along and cover him.

"I will not live this way!" he cried to the wind. "I will not be small and weak and poor. I will be a king, a warrior . . . or I will not be at all."

And then it seemed that the sound of the waves turned to a deep-voiced lullaby, and Theseus fell asleep—not quite asleep, perhaps, because he was watching a great white gull smashing clams open by dropping them on the rocks below. Then the bird swooped down and stood near Theseus' head looking at him, and spoke, "I can crack clams open because they are heavy. Can I do this with shrimps or scallops? No . . . they are too light. Do you know the answer to my riddle?"

"Is it a riddle?"

"A very important one. The answer is this: do not fear your enemy's size, but use it against him. Then his strength will become yours. When you have tried this secret, come back, and I will tell you a better one."

Theseus sat up, rubbing his eyes. Was it a dream? Had the gull been there, speaking to him? Could it be? What did it all mean? Theseus thought and thought; then he leaped to his feet and raced down the beach, up the cliff to the village where he found the boy who had just beaten him and slapped him across the face. When the boy, who was almost as big as a man, lunged toward him swinging his big fist, Theseus caught the fist and pulled in the same direction. The boy, swung off balance by his own power, went spinning off his feet and landed headfirst.

"Get up," said Theseus. "I want to try that again."

The big fellow lumbered to his feet and rushed at Theseus, who stooped suddenly. The boy went hurtling over him and landed in the road again. This time he lay still.

"Well," said Theseus, "that was a smart gull."

One by one, Theseus challenged the largest boys of the village; and, by being swift and sure and using their own strength against them, he defeated them all.

Then, he returned to the beach and lay on the sand, watching the waves, and listening as the crashing became a lullaby. Once again, his eyes closed, then opened. The great white seagull was pacing the sand near him.

"Thank you," said Theseus.

"Don't thank me," said the gull. "Thank your father. I am but his messenger."

"My father, the king?"

"King, indeed. But not the king your mother thinks."

"What do you mean?"

"Listen now . . . Your father rules no paltry stretch of earth. His domain is as vast as all the seas, and all that is beneath them, and all that the seas claim. He is the Earthshaker, Poseidon."

"Poseidon . . . my father?"

"You are his son."

"Then why does my mother not know? How can this be?"

"You must understand, boy, that the gods sometimes fall in love with beautiful maidens of the earth, but they cannot appear to the maidens in their own forms. The gods are too large, too bright, too terrifying, so they must disguise themselves. Now, when Poseidon fell in love with your mother, she had just been secretly married to Aegeus, king of Athens. Poseidon disguised himself as her new husband, and you, you are his son. One of many, very many; but he seems to have taken a special fancy to you and plans great and terrible things for you . . . if you have the courage."

"I have the courage," said Theseus. "Let me know his will."

"Tomorrow," said the seagull, "you will receive an unexpected gift. Then you must bid farewell to your mother and go to Athens to visit Aegeus. Do not go by sea. Take the dangerous overland route, and your adventures will begin."

The waves made great crashing music. The wind

crooned. A blackness crossed the boy's mind. When he opened his eyes the gull was gone, and the sun was dipping into the sea.

"Undoubtedly a dream," he said to himself. "But the last dream worked. Perhaps this one will too."

The next morning there was a great excitement in the village. A huge stone had appeared in the middle of the road. In this stone was stuck a sword half-way up to its hilt; and a messenger had come from the oracle at Delphi saying that whoever pulled the sword from the stone was a king's son and must go to his father.

When Theseus heard this, he embraced his mother and said, "Farewell."

"Where are you going, my son?"

"To Athens. This is the time we have been waiting for. I shall take the sword from the stone and be on my way."

"But, son, it is sunk so deeply. Do you think you can? Look . . . look . . . the strongest men cannot budge it. There is the smith trying . . . And there the Captain of the Guard . . . And look . . . look at that giant herdsman trying. See how he pulls and grunts. Oh, son, I fear the time is not yet."

"Pardon me," said Theseus, moving through the crowd. "Let me through, please. I should like a turn."

When the villagers heard this, heard the short fragile-looking youth say these words, they exploded in laughter.

"Delighted to amuse you," said Theseus. "Now, watch this."

Theseus grasped the sword by the hilt and drew it from the stone as easily as though he were drawing it from a scabbard; he bowed to the crowd and stuck the sword in his belt. The villagers were too stunned to say anything. They moved apart as he approached, making room for him to pass. He smiled, embraced his mother again, and set out on the long road to Athens.

THE ROAD

The overland road from Troezen to Athens was the most dangerous in the world. It was infested not only by bandits but also giants, ogres, and sorcerers who lay in wait for travelers and killed them for their money, or their weapons, or just for sport. Those who had to make the trip usually went by boat, preferring the risk of ship-wreck and pirates to the terrible mountain brigands. If the trip overland had to be made, travelers banded to-gether, went heavily armed, and kept watch as though on a military march.

Theseus knew all this, but he did not give it a second thought. He was too happy to be on his way . . . leaving his poky little village and his ordinary life. He was off to the great world and adventure. He welcomed the dangers that lay in wait. "The more, the better," he thought. "Where there's danger, there's glory. Why, I shall be disappointed if I am *not* attacked."

He was not to be disappointed. He had not gone far when he met a huge man in a bearskin carrying an enor-mous brass club. This was Corynetes, the cudgeler, ter-ror of travelers. He reached out a hairy hand, seized Theseus by the throat and lifted his club, which glit-tered in the hot sunlight.

"Pardon me," said Theseus. "What are you planning to do?"

"Bash in your head."

"Why?"

"That's what I do."

"A beautiful club you have there, sir," said Theseus. "So bright and shiny. You know, it's a positive honor to have my head bashed in with a weapon like this."

"Pure brass," growled the bandit.

"Mmm . . . but is it really brass? It might be gilded wood, you know. A brass club would be too heavy to lift."

"Not too heavy for me," said the bandit, "and it's pure brass. Look . . ."

He held out his club, which Theseus accepted, smiling. Swinging it in a mighty arc he cracked the bandit's head as if it were an egg.

"Nice balance to this," said Theseus. "I think I'll keep it." He shouldered the club and walked off.

The road ran along the edge of the cliff above the burning blue sea. He turned a bend in the road and saw a man sitting on a rock. The man held a great battle-ax in his hand; he was so large that the ax seemed more like a hatchet.

"Stop!" said the man.

"Good day," said Theseus.

"Now listen, stranger, everyone who passes this way washes my feet. That's the toll. Any questions?"

"One. Suppose I don't?"

"Then I'll simply cut off your head," said the man, "unless you think that little twig you're carrying will stop this ax."

"I was just asking," said Theseus. "I'll be glad to wash your feet, sir. Personal hygiene is very important, especially on the road."

"What?"

"I said I'll do it."

Theseus knelt at the man's feet and undid his sandals, thinking hard. He knew who this man was; he had heard tales of him. This was Sciron who was notorious

for keeping a pet turtle that was as large for a turtle as
Sciron was for a man and was trained to eat human
flesh. This giant turtle swam about at the foot of
the cliff waiting for Sciron to kick his victims over.
Theseus glanced swiftly down the cliffside. Sure
enough, he saw the great blunt head of the turtle lifted
out of the water, waiting.

Theseus took Sciron's huge foot in his hand, holding
it by the ankle. As he did so, the giant launched a
mighty kick. Theseus was ready. When the giant
kicked, Theseus pulled, dodging swiftly out of the way
as the enormous body hurtled over him, over and down,
splashing the water cliff-high as it hit. Theseus saw the
turtle swim toward the splash. He arose, dusted off his
knees, and proceeded on his journey.

The road dipped now, running past a grove of pines.
"Stop!"

He stopped. There was another huge brute of a
man facing him. First Theseus thought that Sciron had
climbed back up the cliff somehow; but then he realized
that this must be Sciron's brother, of whom he had
also heard. This fellow was called Pityocamptes, which
means "pine-bender." He was big enough and strong
enough to press pine trees to the ground. It was his habit
to bend a tree just as a passerby approached and asked
the newcomer to hold it for a moment. The traveler,
afraid not to oblige, would grasp the top of the tree. Then
Pityocamptes with a great jeering laugh would release
his hold. The pine tree would spring mightily to its
full height, flinging the victim high in the air, so high
that the life was dashed out of him when he hit the
ground. Then the bandit would search his pockets,
chuckling all the while; he was a great joker. Now he
said to Theseus, "Wait, friend. I want you to do me
a favor."

He reached for a pine tree and bent it slowly to earth

like an enormous bow. "Just hold this for a moment like a good fellow, will you?"

"Certainly," said Theseus.

Theseus grasped the tree, set his feet, clenched his teeth, let his mind go dark and all his strength flow downward, through his legs, into the earth, anchoring him to the earth like a rock. Pityocamptes let go, expecting to see Theseus fly into the air. Nothing happened. The pine stayed bent. The lad was holding it, legs rigid, arms trembling. The giant could not believe his eyes. He thought he must have broken the pine while bending it. He leaned his head closer to see. Then Theseus let go. The tree snapped up, catching the giant under the chin, knocking him unconscious. Theseus bent the tree again, swiftly bound the giant's wrists to it. He pulled down another pine and tied Pityocamptes' legs to that . . . and then let both pines go. They sprang apart. Half of Pityocamptes hung from one tree, half from the other. Vultures screamed with joy and fed on both parts impartially. Theseus wiped the pine tar from his hands and continued on his way.

By now it was nightfall, and he was very weary. He came to an inn where light was coming from the window, smoke from the chimney. But it was not a cozy sight; the front yard was littered with skulls and other bones.

"They don't do much to attract guests," thought Theseus. "Well . . . I'm tired. It has been a gruesome day. I'd just as soon go to bed now without any more fighting. On the other hand, if an adventure comes my way, I must not avoid it. Let's see what this bone-collector looks like."

He strode to the door and pounded on it, crying, "Landlord! Landlord, ho!"

The door flew open. In it was framed a greasy-looking giant, resembling Sciron and the pine-bender, but older, filthier, with long, tangled gray hair and a blood-stained gray beard. He had great meaty hands like grappling hooks.

"Do you have a bed for the night?" said Theseus.

"A bed? That I have. Come with me."

He led Theseus to a room where a bed stood—an enormous ugly piece of furniture, hung with leather straps, and chains, and shackles.

"What are all those bolts and bindings for?" said Theseus.

"To keep you in bed until you've had your proper rest."

"Why should I wish to leave the bed?"

"Everyone else seems to. You see, this is a special bed, exactly six feet long from head to foot. And I am a very neat, orderly person. I like things to fit. Now, if the guest is too short for the bed, we attach those chains to his ankles and stretch him. Simple."

"And if he's too long?" said Theseus.

"Oh, well then we just lop off his legs to the proper length."

"I see."

"But don't worry about that part of it. You look like a stretch job to me. Go ahead, lie down."

"And if I do, then you will attach chains to my ankles and stretch me—if I understand you correctly."

"You understand me fine. Lie down."

"But all this stretching sounds uncomfortable."

"You came here. Nobody invited you. Now you've got to take the bad with the good."

"Yes, of course," said Theseus. "I suppose if I decided not to take advantage of your hospitality . . . I suppose you'd *make* me lie down, wouldn't you?"

"Oh, sure. No problem."

"How? Show me."

The inn-keeper, whose name was Procrustes, reached out a great hand, put it on Theseus' chest, and pushed him toward the bed. Theseus took his wrist, and, as the big man pushed, he pulled . . . in the swift shoulder-turning downward snap he had taught himself. Procrustes flew over his shoulder and landed on the bed. Theseus bolted him fast, took up an ax, and chopped off his legs as they dangled over the footboards. Then, because he did not wish the fellow to suffer, chopped off his head too.

"As you have done by travelers, so are you done by," said Theseus. "You have made your bed, old man. Now lie on it."

He put down the ax, picked up his club, and resumed his journey, deciding to sleep in the open because he found the inn unpleasant.

ATHENS

Athens was not yet a great city in those days, but it was far more splendid than any Theseus had seen. He found it quite beautiful with arbors and terraces and marble temples. After the adventures of the road, however, he found it strangely dull. He suffered too from humiliation for, although he was the king's son, his father was in a very weak position so he could not be a real prince. It was his father's powerful cousin, the tall blackbrowed Pallas with his fifty fierce sons, who actually ran things. Their estate was much larger and finer than the castle, their private army stronger than the Royal Guard, and Theseus could not bear it.

"Why was I given the sign?" he stormed. "Why did I pull the sword from the stone and come here to Athens? To skulk in the castle like a runaway slave? What difference does it make, Father, how *many* there are? After we fight them, there will be many less. Let's fight! Right now!"

"No," said Aegeus, "we cannot. Not yet. It would not be a battle, it would be suicide. They must not know you are here. I am sorry now I had you come all the way to Athens. It is too dangerous. I should have kept you in some little village somewhere, outside of town, where we could have seen each other every day, but where you would not be in such danger."

"Well, if I am no use here let me go to Crete!" cried Theseus. "If I can't fight our enemies at home, let me try my hand abroad."

"Crete! . . . Oh, my dear boy, no, no . . ." and the old man fell to lamenting for it was in these days that Athens, defeated in a war with Crete, was forced by King Minos to pay a terrible tribute. He demanded that each year the Athenians send him seven of their most beautiful maidens, seven of their strongest young men. These were taken to the Labyrinth and offered to the monster who lived there—the dread Minotaur, half man and half bull—son of Pasiphae and the bull she had fallen in love with. Year after year they were taken from their parents, these seven maidens and seven youths, and were never heard of again. Now the day of tribute was approaching again.

Theseus offered to go himself as one of the seven young men and take his chances with the monster. He kept hammering at his father, kept producing so many arguments, was so electric with impatience and rage, that finally his father consented, and the name Theseus was entered among those who were to be selected for tribute. The night before he left, he embraced Aegeus and said, "Be of good heart, dear sire. I traveled a road that was supposed to be fatal before and came out alive. I met quite a few unpleasant characters on my journey and had a few anxious moments, but I learned from them that the best weapon you can give an enemy is your own fear. So . . . who can tell. I may emerge victorious from the Labyrinth and lead my companions home safely. Then I will be known to the people of Athens and will be able to rouse them against your tyrant cousins and make you a real king."

"May the gods protect you, son," said Aegeus. "I shall sacrifice to Zeus and to Ares, and to our own Athene, every day, and pray for your safety."

"Don't forget Poseidon," said Theseus.

"Oh, yes, Poseidon too," said Aegeus. "Now do this for me, son. Each day I shall climb the Hill of the Temple, and from there watch over the sea . . . watching for your ship to return. It will depart wearing black sails, as all the sad ships of tribute do; but if you should overcome the Minotaur, please, I pray you, raise a white sail. This will tell me that you are alive and save a day's vigil."

"That I will do," said Theseus. "Watch for the white sail . . ."

CRETE

All Athens was at the pier to see the black-sailed ship depart. The parents of the victims were weeping and tearing their clothing. The maidens and the young men, chosen for their beauty and courage, stood on the deck trying to look proud; but the sound of lamentation reached them, and they wept to see their parents weep. Then Theseus felt the cords of his throat tighten with rage. He stamped his foot on the deck and shouted, "Up anchor, and away!" as though he were the captain of the vessel. The startled crew obeyed, and the ship moved out of the harbor.

Theseus immediately called the others to him.

"Listen to me," he said. "You are not to look upon your-selves as victims, or victims you will surely be. The time of tribute has ended. You are to regard this voyage not as a submission but as a military expedition. Every-thing will change, but first you must change your own way of looking at things. Place your faith in my hands, place yourselves under my command. Will you?"

"We will!" they shouted.

"Good. Now I want every man to instruct every girl in the use of the sword and the battle-ax. We may have to cut our way to freedom. I shall also train you to re-spond to my signals—whistles, hand-movements—for if we work as a team, we may be able to defeat the Minotaur and confound our enemies."

They agreed eagerly. They were too young to live without hope, and Theseus' words filled them with courage. Every day he drilled them, man and maiden alike, as though they were a company of soldiers. He taught them to wrestle in the way he had invented. And this wild young activity, this sparring and fencing, so excited the crew, that they were eager to place them-selves under the young man's command.

"Yes," he said. "I will take your pledges. You are Athenians. Right now that means you are poor, de-feated, living in fear. But one day 'Athenian' will be the proudest name in the world, a word to make war-riors quake in their armor, kings shiver upon their thrones!"

Now Minos of Crete was the most powerful king in all the world. His capital, Knossos, was the gayest, richest, proudest city in the world; and the day, each year, when the victims of the Minotaur arrived from Athens, was always a huge feast-day. People mobbed the streets—warriors with shaven heads and gorgeous feathered cloaks, women in jewels and topless dresses, children, farmers, great swaggering bullherders, lithe bullfighters, dwarfs, peacocks, elephants, and slaves, slaves, slaves from every country known to man. The streets were so jammed no one could walk freely, but the King's Guard kept a lane open from quayside to Palace. And here, each year, the fourteen victims were marched so that the whole city could see them—marched past the crowds to the Palace to be presented to the king to have their beauty approved before giving them to the Minotaur.

On this day of arrival, the excited harbormaster came puffing to the castle, fell on his knees before the throne, and gasped, "Pity, great king, pity . . ."

And then in a voice strangled with fright the harbormaster told the king that one of the intended victims, a young man named Theseus, demanded a private audience with Minos before he would allow the Athenians to disembark.

"My warships!" thundered Minos. "The harbor is full of triremes. Let the ship be seized, and this Theseus and his friends dragged here through the streets."

"It cannot be, your majesty. Their vessel stands over the narrow neck of the harbor. And he swears to scuttle it right there, blocking the harbor, if any of our ships approach."

"Awkward . . . very awkward," murmured Minos. "Quite resourceful for an Athenian, this young man. Worth taking a look at. Let him be brought to me."

Thereupon Theseus was informed that the king agreed to see him privately. He was led to the Palace, looking about eagerly as he was ushered down the lane past the enormous crowd. He had never seen a city like this. It made Athens look like a little fishing village. He was excited and he walked proudly, head high, eyes flashing. When he came to the Palace, he was introduced to the king's daughters, two lovely young princesses, Ariadne and Phaedra.

"I regret that my queen is not here to greet you," said Minos. "But she has become attached to her summer house in the Labyrinth and spends most of her time there."

The princesses were silent, but they never took their eyes off Theseus. He could not decide which one he preferred. Ariadne he supposed—the other was really still a little girl. But she had a curious cat-faced look about her that intrigued him. However, he could not give much thought to this; his business was with the king.

Finally, Minos signaled the girls to leave the room, and motioned Theseus toward his throne. "You wanted to see me alone," he said. "Here I am. Speak."

"I have a request, your majesty. As the son of my father, Aegeus, King of Athens, and his representative in this court, I ask you formally to stop demanding your yearly tribute."

"Oh, heavens," said Minos. "I thought you would have something original to say. And you come with this threadbare old petition. I have heard it a thousand times and refused it a thousand times."

"I know nothing of what has been done before," said Theseus. "But only of what I must do. You laid this tribute upon Athens to punish the city, to show the world that you were the master. But it serves only to degrade you and show the world that you are a fool."

"Feeding you to the Minotaur is much too pleasant a finale for such an insolent rascal," said Minos. "I shall think of a much more interesting way for you to die— perhaps several ways."

"Let me explain what I mean," said Theseus. "Strange as it seems, I do not hate you. I admire you. You're the most powerful king in the world and I admire power. In fact, I intend to imitate your career. So what I say, I say in all friendliness, and it is this: when you take our young men and women and shut them in the Labyrinth to be devoured by the Minotaur, you are making the whole world forget Minos, the great general Minos, the wise king. What you are forcing upon their attention is Minos, the betrayed husband, the man whose wife disliked him so much she eloped with a bull. And this image of you is what people remember. Drop the tribute, I say, and you will once again live in man's mind as warrior, law-giver, and king."

"You are an agile debater," said Minos, "as well as a very reckless young man, saying these things to me. But there is a flaw in your argument. If I were to drop the tribute, my subjects would construe this as an act of weakness. They would be encouraged to launch conspiracies against me. Other countries under my sway would be encouraged to rebel. It cannot be done."

"I can show you a graceful way to let the tribute lapse. One that will not be seen as a sign of weakness. Just tell me how to kill the monster."

"Kill the monster, eh? And return to Athens a hero? And wipe out your enemies there? And then subdue the other cities of Greece until you become leader of a great alliance? And then come visit me again with a huge fleet and an enormous army, and topple old Minos from his throne . . . ? Do I describe your ambitions correctly?"

"The future does not concern me," said Theseus. "I take one thing at a time. And the thing that interests me now is killing the Minotaur."

"Oh, forget the Minotaur," said Minos. "How do you know there is one? How do you know it's not some maniac there who ties sticks to his head? Whatever it is, let him rot there in the Labyrinth with his mad mother. I have a better plan for you. My sons are dead. My daughter Ariadne, I notice, looks upon you with favor. Marry her, and become my heir. One day you will rule Crete and Athens both . . . and all the cities of the sea."

"Thank you, sir. I appreciate your offer. But I came here to fight a monster."

"You are mad."

"Perhaps. But this is the only way I know how to be. When I am your age, when the years have thinned my blood, when rage has cooled into judgment, then I will go in for treaties, compromises. Now, I must fight."

"Why is the young fool so confident?" thought Minos to himself. "He acts like a man who knows he is protected by the gods. Can it be true what they say? Is he really the son of Poseidon? Do I have that kind of enemy on my hands? If so, I will make doubly sure to get rid of him."

Then he said aloud, "You are wrong to refuse my offer. I suppose you are made so wildly rash by some old wives' gossip in your little village that you are the son of this god or that. Those mountain villages of yours, they're ridiculous. Every time a child does something out of the way, all the crones and hags get together and whisper, 'He's the son of a god, really the son of a god.' Is that the way of it? Tell the truth now."

"My truth," said Theseus, "is that I am the son of Poseidon."

"Poseidon, eh? No less. Well, how would you like to prove it?"

"Why should I care to prove it? *I* know. That's enough for me. The whole world has heard that you are the son of Zeus, who courted your mother, Europa, in the guise of a white bull. Everyone has heard this tale; few disbelieve it. But can you prove it?"

"Come with me," said Minos.

He led him out of the Palace, beyond the wall, to a cliff overlooking the sea. He stood tall, raised his arms, and said, "Father Zeus, make me a sign."

Lightning flashed so furiously that the night became brighter than day, and the sky spoke in thunder. Then Minos dropped his arms; the light stopped pulsing in the sky, and the thunder was still.

"Well," said Minos. "Have I proved my parentage?"

"It's an impressive display. I suppose it proves something."

"Then show me you are the son of Poseidon."

Minos took the crown from his head and threw it over the cliff into the sea. They heard the tiny splash far below.

"If you are his son, the sea holds no terror for you. Get me my crown," said Minos.

Without a moment's hesitation, Theseus stepped to the edge of the cliff and leaped off. As he fell, he murmured, "Father, help me now."

Down he plunged, struck the black water and went under, shearing his way through until he felt his lungs bursting. But he did not kick toward the surface. He let out the air in his chest in a long tortured gasp, and then, breathed in. No strangling rush of water, but a great lung-full of sweet cool air . . . and he felt himself breathing as naturally as a fish. He swam down, down, and as he swam his eyes became accustomed to the color of the night sea; he moved in a deep green light. And the first thing he saw was the crown gleaming on the bottom. He swam down and picked it up.

Theseus stood on the ocean bottom holding the crown in his hand and said, "All thanks, Father Poseidon."

He waited there for the god to answer him, but all he saw were dark gliding shapes, creatures of the sea passing like shadows. He swam slowly to the surface, climbed the cliff, and walked to where Minos was waiting.

"Your crown, sir."

"Thank you."

"Are you convinced now that Poseidon is my father?"

"I am convinced that the water is more shallow here than I thought. Convinced that you are lucky."

"Luck? Is that not another word for divine favor?"

"Perhaps. At any rate, I am also convinced that you are a dangerous young man. So dangerous that I am forced to strip you of certain advantages allowed those who face the Minotaur. You will carry neither sword nor ax, but only your bare hands . . . And your luck, of course. I think we will not meet again. So farewell." He whistled sharply. His Royal Guard appeared, surrounded Theseus, and marched him off to a stone tower at the edge of the Labyrinth. There they locked him up for the night.

An hour before dawn Ariadne appeared in his cell and said, "I love you, Theseus. I will save you from death if you promise to take me back to Athens with you."

"And how do you propose to save me, lovely princess?"

"Do you know what the Labyrinth is? It is a hedge of a thousand lanes, all leading in, and only one leading out. And this one is so concealed, has so many twists and turns and secret windings that no one can possibly find his way out. Only I can travel the Labyrinth freely. I will lead you in and hide you. I will also lead you around the central chamber where the Minotaur is and lead you out again. You will not even see the monster. Since no one has ever found his way out of the maze, Minos will assume that you have killed the Minotaur, and you will have a chance to get to your ship and escape before the trick is discovered. But you must take me with you."

"It cannot be," said Theseus.

"Don't you believe me? It's all true. Look . . ."

She took from her tunic a ball of yellow silk thread and dropped it on the floor. The ball swiftly rolled across the room, unwinding itself as it went. It rolled around the bench, wrapped itself around one of Theseus' ankles, rolled up the wall, across the ceiling and down again. Then Ariadne tugged sharply on her end of the thread, and the ball reversed itself, rolling back the way it had come, reeling in its thread as it rolled. Back to Ariadne it rolled and leaped into her hand.

"This was made for me by old Daedalus," said Ariadne. "It was he who built the Labyrinth, you know. And my father shut him up in it too. I used to go visit him there. He made me this magic ball of thread so that I would always be able to find my way to him, and find my way back. He was very fond of me."

"I'm getting very fond of you too," said Theseus.

"Do you agree?" cried Ariadne. "Will you let me guide you in the Labyrinth and teach you how to avoid the monster, and fool my father. Say you will. Please . . ."

"I'll let you guide me through the maze," said Theseus. "Right to where the monster dwells. You can stay there and watch the fight. And when it's over, you can lead me back."

"No, no, I won't be able to. You'll be dead! It's impossible for you to fight the Minotaur."

"It is impossible for me not to."

"You won't even be armed."

"I have always traveled light, sweet princess, and taken my weapons from the enemy. I see no reason to change my habits now. Are you the kind of girl who seeks to change a man's habits? If you are, I don't think I will take you back to Athens."

"Oh, please, do not deny me your love," she said. "I will do as you say."

———

The next morning when the Royal Guard led Theseus out of the tower and forced him into the outer lane of the Labyrinth, Ariadne was around the first bend, waiting. She tied one end of the thread to a branch of the hedge, then dropped the ball to the ground. It rolled slowly, unwinding; they followed, hand in hand. It was pleasant, walking in the Labyrinth. The hedge grew tall above their heads and was heavy with little white sweet-smelling flowers. The lane turned and twisted and turned again, but the ball of thread ran ahead, and they followed it. Theseus heard a howling.

"Sounds like the wind," he said.

"No, it is not the wind. It is my mad mother, howling."

They walked farther. They heard a rumbling, crashing sound.

"What's that?"

"That is my brother. He's hungry."

They continued to follow the ball of thread. Now the hedges grew so tall the branches met above their heads, and it was dark. Ariadne looked up at him, sadly. He bent his head and brushed her lips in a kiss.

"Please don't go to him," she said. "Let me lead you out now. He will kill you. He has the strength of a bull and the cunning of a man."

"Who knows?" said Theseus. "Perhaps he has the weakness of a man and the stupidity of a bull." He put his hand over her mouth. "Anyway, let me think so because I must fight him, you see, and I'd rather not frighten myself beforehand."

The horrid roaring grew louder and louder. The ball of thread ran ahead, ran out of the lane, into an open space. And here, in a kind of meadow surrounded by the tall hedges of the Labyrinth, stood the Minotaur.

Theseus could not believe his eyes. The thing was more fearsome than in his worst dreams. What he had expected was a bull's head on a man's body. What he saw was something about ten feet tall shaped like a man, like an incredibly huge and brutally muscular man, but covered with a short dense brown fur. It had a man's face, but a squashed, bestialized one, with poisonous red eyes, great blunt teeth, and thin leathery lips. Sprouting out of its head were two long heavy polished horns. Its feet were hooves, razor sharp; its hands were shaped like a man's hands, but much larger and hard as horn. When it clenched them they were great fists of bone.

It stood pawing the grass with a hoof, peering at Theseus with its little red eyes. There was a bloody slaver on its lips.

Now, for the first time in all his battles, Theseus became unsure of himself. He was confused by the appearance of the monster. It filled him with a kind of horror that was beyond fear, as if he were wrestling a giant spider. So when the monster lowered its head and charged, thrusting those great bone lances at him, Theseus could not move out of the way.

There was only one thing to do. Drawing himself up on tiptoe, making himself as narrow as possible, he leaped into the air and seized the monster's horns. Swinging himself between the horns, he somersaulted onto the Minotaur's head, where he crouched, gripping the horns with desperate strength. The monster bellowed with rage and shook its head violently. But Theseus held on. He thought his teeth would shake out of his head; he felt his eyeballs rattling in their sockets. But he held on.

Now, if it can be done without one's being gored, somersaulting between the horns is an excellent tactic when fighting a real bull; but the Minotaur was not a real bull; it had hands. So when Theseus refused to be

shaken off but stood on the head between the horns trying to dig his heels into the beast's eyes, the Minotaur
stopped shaking his head, closed his great horny fist,
big as a cabbage and hard as a rock, and struck a vicious backward blow, smashing his fist down on his
head, trying to squash Theseus as you squash a beetle.

This is what Theseus was waiting for. As soon as the
fist swung toward him, he jumped off the Minotaur's
head, and the fist smashed between the horns, full on
the skull. The Minotaur's knees bent, he staggered and
fell over; he had stunned himself. Theseus knew he had
only a few seconds before the beast would recover his
strength. He rushed to the monster, took a horn in both
hands, put his foot against the ugly face, and putting all
his strength in a sudden tug, broke the horn off at the
base. He leaped away. Now he, too, was armed, and
with a weapon taken from the enemy.

The pain of the breaking horn goaded the Minotaur
out of his momentary swoon. He scrambled to his feet,
uttered a great choked bellow, and charged toward
Theseus, trying to hook him with his single horn. Bone
cracked against bone as Theseus parried with his horn.
It was like a duel now, the beast thrusting with his
horn, Theseus parrying, thrusting in return. Since the
Minotaur was much stronger, it forced Theseus back—
back until it had Theseus pinned against the hedge. As
soon as he felt the first touch of the hedge, Theseus dis-
engaged, ducked past the Minotaur, and raced to the
center of the meadow, where he stood, poised, arm
drawn back. For the long pointed horn made as good a
javelin as it did a sword, and so could be used at a safer
distance.

The Minotaur whirled and charged again. Theseus
waited until he was ten paces away, and then whipped
his arm forward, hurling the javelin with all his
strength. It entered the bull's neck and came out the

other side. But so powerful was the Minotaur's rush, so stubborn his bestial strength, that he trampled on with the sharp horn through his neck and ran right over Theseus, knocking him violently to the ground. Then it whirled to try to stab Theseus with its horn; but the blood was spouting fast now, and the monster staggered and fell on the ground beside Theseus.

Ariadne ran to the fallen youth. She turned him over, raised him in her arms; he was breathing. She kissed him. He opened his eyes, looked around, and saw the dead Minotaur; then he looked back at her and smiled. He climbed to his feet, leaning heavily on Ariadne.

"Tell your thread to wind itself up again, Princess. We're off to Athens."

When Theseus came out of the Labyrinth there was an enormous crowd of Cretans gathered. They had heard the sound of fighting, and, as the custom was, had gathered to learn of the death of the hostages. When they saw the young man covered with dirt and blood, carrying a broken horn, with Ariadne clinging to his arm, they raised a great shout.

Minos was there, standing with his arms folded. Phaedra was at his side. Theseus bowed to him and said, "Your majesty, I have the honor to report that I have rid your kingdom of a foul monster."

"Prince Theseus," said Minos. "According to the terms of the argeement, I must release you and your fellow hostages."

"Your daughter helped me, king. I have promised to take her with me. Have you any objection?"

"I fancy it is too late for objections. The women of our family haven't had much luck in these matters. Try not to be too beastly to her."

"Father," said Phaedra, "she will be lonesome there

in far-off Athens. May I not go with her and keep her company?"

"You too?" said Minos. He turned to Theseus. "Truly, young man, whether or not Poseidon has been working for you, Aphrodite surely has."

"I will take good care of your daughters, king," said Theseus. "Farewell."

And so, attended by the Royal Guard, Theseus, his thirteen happy companions, and the two Cretan princesses, walked through the mobbed streets from the Palace to the harbor. There they boarded their ship.

It was a joyous ship that sailed northward from Crete to Athens. There was feasting and dancing night and day. And every young man aboard felt himself a hero too, and every maiden a princess. And Theseus was lord of them all, drunk with strength and joy. He was so happy he forgot his promise to his father—forgot to tell the crew to take down the black sail and raise a white one.

King Aegeus, keeping a lonely watch on the Hill of the Temple, saw first a tiny speck on the horizon. He watched it for a long time and saw it grow big and then bigger. He could not tell whether the sail was white or black; but as it came nearer, his heart grew heavy. The sail seemed to be dark. The ship came nearer, and he saw that it wore a black sail. He knew that his son was dead.

"I have killed him," he cried. "In my weakness, I sent him off to be killed. I am unfit to be king, unfit to live. I must go to Tartarus immediately and beg his pardon there."

And the old king leaped from the hill, dived through the steep air into the sea far below, and was drowned. He gave that lovely blue, fatal stretch of water its name for all time—the Aegean Sea.

Theseus, upon his return to Athens, was hailed as king. The people worshipped him. He swiftly raised an army, wiped out his powerful cousins, and then led the Athenians forth into many battles, binding all the cities of Greece together in an alliance. Then, one day he returned to Crete to reclaim the crown of Minos which once he had recovered from the sea.

Atalanta

Atalanta's bad luck began when she was born, for her father, the king of Arcadia, wanted a son. In his rage at being given a girl, he ordered that she be left on a mountainside to die. The nearest mountain, as it happened, was in the neighboring country of Calydon so the infant girl was taken there. She was stuck in a cleft of rock and left under the cold stars.

Her cries attracted the attention of a she-bear who

was prowling the slope looking for a lost cub. The huge blunt-headed furry beast came nosing up to the squalling infant. It was not her cub, but it was alive; its tiny hand came out and clutched the shaggy ruff of the bear. She lifted the baby gently in her jaws and carried it off to her cave.

Across the valley from the she-bear's cave stood a castle belonging to the king of Calydon, whose son named Meleager also had a curious infancy. When he was three days old, his mother, Queen Althaea, was visited by a tall, gray-faced old woman carrying a pair of long silver shears in her hand. The queen knew it was Atropos, one of the three Fates, and she was afraid. The old woman said to her, "We are being kind to you. We usually strike without warning. See that stick of wood at the edge of the fire, just beginning to burn? Your son's life will last just as long as that stick remains unburned."

Atropos then disappeared.

Althaea leaped to the fireplace, snatched the stick out of the flames, and locked it in a great brass chest.

The prince was not the same as other children; from the time he could run he was interested in nothing but hunting. His father was delighted with the boy. He had his smith make a tiny spear and a bow that shot arrows no larger than darts, but they were not toys. Meleager practiced with them constantly and learned to use them well. As soon as he could sit on a pony, he followed his father on the hunt; and by the time he was a young man, he was accounted the best hunter in all Greece. He had taken enough pelts to cover the floors of the huge castle . . . skin of lion, wolf, and bear. The walls were hung with stag-horns and bear-tusks. He hunted on horseback in the lowlands; on foot among the hills.

However, Meleager was a worry to his parents in one respect because he snubbed all the eligible maidens of Calydon.

"Father, please," he said. "I can't stand them . . . soft, squealing little things; no good with spear or bow, hopeless on horseback. I'll not marry until I find a girl who can hunt by my side."

One day, on the slope of a near mountain, he cornered an enormous bear. It lashed out with its great paw and struck Meleager's javelin from his hand. Then the bear charged so swiftly that the lad barely had time to draw his dagger before the beast was upon him. He slipped under the swinging paws and stabbed the bear in the back of its neck, and then was knocked off his feet by its backward lurch. As he sprang up, he was just in time to see the bear charging away up the slope, the dagger still stuck in his neck, blood welling from the wound. Meleager scrambled after it.

Despite his terrible wound, the beast moved swiftly, and Meleager soon lost sight of him; but he followed the trail of blood, knowing that it was only a question of time till the animal dropped. It had been early morning when he fought the bear; now the burning summer sun was directly overhead, and he was panting with heat as he followed the trail of blood. Then, rounding a spur of rock, he saw an amazing sight: a tall, bare-legged maiden came running down the hill with long strides, wearing a great shaggy fur cloak. Just as he thought, "Why is she wearing that heavy cloak in all this heat?" he saw that blood was dripping from her and realized that it was not a fur cloak she was wearing, but that on her back was the huge bear he had fought. The animal's head was lolling on her shoulder, its blood was dripping on her; he saw the hilt of his dagger still protruding from its neck.

He stood in the path. The girl stopped. Gently she

slid the body of the bear to the ground, straightened, and faced him. He was dazed by her beauty. She was as tall as he, long-legged as a deer, clad in a brief tunic of wolf-skin, her rich brown hair hanging to her thighs. Her face was streaked with dirt, her bare arms and shoulders blotched with blood; he knew instantly that this was the one girl in the world for him.

"That's my bear," he said. "But I give him to you."

"Your bear?"

"My kill. That's my dagger sticking from his neck. I've been tracking him all day. But you can . . ."

He was interrupted by her hoarse cry of rage. She stooped swiftly, picked up a huge stone as if it were a pebble, and hurled it at his head. He ducked but felt it graze his hair. He saw her bend again and pull his dagger from the bear's neck. Then, holding the dagger, she came slowly toward him.

"This bear is my brother," she said. "You have killed my brother. Now I must kill you."

"Sweet maiden . . ."

"Sweet? You'll find me bitter as death. Come, pick up your spear and fight."

He picked up his spear and hurled it in the same motion. It sang through the air and split a sapling neatly in two. He turned and stood facing her with empty hands.

"Why have you disarmed yourself?" she said. "I mean to kill you."

"Come ahead then. Use the dagger, by all means. It will make things more even."

She howled with rage, and flung the dagger away. "I need no favors from you!" she cried. "I'll do it with my bare hands."

She rushed upon him. He caught her by the arms and tried to handle her gently; but it was impossible as she was as strong as a wild mare. She caught him in a great bear-hug that almost cracked his spine. Grunting, twisting, he broke her hold and then wresfled in earnest. There, under the hot sun, before the glassy dead eyes of the bear, they wrestled.

Atalanta was a powerful fighter because she had been adopted by the she-bear, raised in the bear's cave, and treated like a cub. She had grown up among successive litters of bear cubs, wrestling with them, hunting with them; she had grown into a gloriously tanned, supple, fleet-footed young woman, strong as a she-bear herself. Wrestling Meleager seemed an easy matter to her. She planned to crush him in her hug and hurl him over the cliff.

However, as she wrestled with Meleager under the hot sun among the fragrance of thyme and crushed grass, something new happened. She had been used to wrestling shaggy bears, noticing with wonder how smooth her own arms and legs seemed against their mass of fur. She had wondered why she was so different, so hairless, and yet glad somehow that she was different. And now, as she held the young man in her mighty clutch, she felt his smoothness; and it was as though she were touching herself for the first time. Her own body seemed strange to her, yet deeply familiar. As she struggled, she found she could no longer know where his body ended and hers began. When she realized this, it seemed to her that the fragrance of the crushed grass rose like a sweet fog, making her dizzy. She found her knees buckling. She who could run miles up the steep slope of a mountain, outrunning even the mountain goats, felt her legs weakening. Her last thought, as her mind swooped and darkened was, "It's magic. He's doing some magic. He's fighting me with magic."

When her head cleared, she found they were sitting

with their backs against a twisted olive tree near the edge of the cliff and looking out onto a great gulf of blueness where a brown eagle turned. Their arms were still about each other as if they were wrestling, but their bodies were still. She was telling her name.

"I am Atalanta. I belong to this mountain, to the clan of mountain bears."

"I am Meleager," he said. "I belong to Atalanta."

So Meleager found the huntress he had dreamed of; they hunted together on hill and lowland, in forest and swamp and field, on foot and horseback, with dogs, or with long-legged hunting cats brought over from Egypt called Cheetahs, but more often, by themselves. They hunted so happily together and brought back so much game that word came to Artemis, Goddess of the Chase, Lady of the Wild Things; word came of Meleager, the handsome prince, the great spearman, and of his companion Atalanta, so tall and fleet and strong that people were saying she was Artemis herself come to earth. The goddess grew very angry.

"I'll show them there is only one Artemis," she cried. "I will set them a hunt they will never forget."

She dug her hands into the muck of the river Scamander and molded a huge boar, mud-colored, with evil red eyes. Far larger than any boar seen by man, large as a rhinoceros, armed with tusks, so long, heavy, and sharp he could shear down a tree with a toss of his head. She made this huge beast, filled him with a raging blood-thirst, and set him in Calydon to ravage the countryside.

THE HUNT

Immediately the beast began to spread death and terror throughout the land. He uprooted crops, killed horses, cattle, goats—and also those who tended them. He attacked men working in the fields, goring and trampling them into bloody rags. And, in a rage, the beast charged a farmhouse, knocking it over, and rooted among the rubble, killing those who had not been crushed by the falling beams. Shepherds and goatherds refused to graze their flocks on the hills; farmers feared to harvest their crops. The king, Meleager's father, was desperate. He asked his son's advice. Meleager was mad with excitement. He swore to his father that he would kill the boar.

"Just I, myself, and one companion. We can do it, Father. No beast can escape us."

But the king said: "No, my son. This is no ordinary beast. It is too large, too irresistibly strong. It is a curse sent by some god whom we have unwittingly offended. Yet I have sacrificed to all the gods, and still the beast roams my poor country, destroying, killing . . ."

"I must hunt him, father! It is the quarry we have dreamed of—something worthy of our skill."

"I forbid it. You are my only son. If you are killed, the country will fall into the hands of your mother's foolish brothers. What we must do, Meleager, is invite all the heroes of Greece to hunt the beast. It will be a famous affair."

Thereupon messages were sent to all the heroes of Hellas, inviting them to Calydon to hunt the giant boar. They all accepted the invitation, kings, princes, and fierce soldiers of fortune who later sailed with Jason and fought at Troy.

However, the old king was not altogether pleased to be playing host to so many great men.

"I shall not be able to join the hunt," he said to his wife. "Meleager will have to do the honors while I stay home and guard the castle."

"Is that necessary?" said the queen. "Don't you trust your neighbors?"

"Yes, I trust them to act like themselves. These neighbors of ours didn't become so rich in land and cattle by right of purchase, my dear. They are men who have always taken when they wanted; this is how they have gained their property and their reputation. Frankly, I fear them more than I do the boar, and yet my heart tells me that my son may die on this hunt and that I should ride with him. I don't know what to do."

"You need not fear for our son," said Queen Althaea. "The Fates have made me the guardian of his life. Look . . ."

She unlocked the chest, showed him the charred brand of wood, and told him how she had been visited by Atropos, Lady of the Shears, who had promised that the prince would live while the brand remained unburned.

"So you may set your mind at rest, dear husband, and let him lead the hunt while you stay home and guard the castle. Besides, I am sending my two brothers to keep an eye on him. No, don't frown. I know your opinion of my brothers, but they are less lenient than you about certain matters. They will prevent him from bringing that wild girl of his to join the hunt."

"It is a mistake to interfere," said the king. "He loves that girl and will never love another."

"He shall not have her!" cried Althaea. "While I draw a breath he shall never bring her home as his wife."

"Well, I can't worry about her at the moment," said the king. "I have more important things on my mind. Fearsome beasts, fearsome guests—the wild girl will have to wait."

"She will wait long before she marries my son," said Althaea.

The next morning, everyone assembled for the hunt. The heroes were amazed when their host, Meleager, rode up with Atalanta at his side. They gazed dumbfounded at the lovely, lithe young huntress, clad in a wolfskin tunic, bow and quiver slung, holding a javelin. A murmur rose. All were surprised; some of them were angry; a few of the younger ones were inflamed by her beauty and grew jealous of Meleager. The prince's solemn uncles rode toward him, beards bristling with outrage.

"It's a disgrace," they said. "You are bringing dishonor on yourself and on your noble guests. They do not wish to ride with this bear's-whelp from the hills."

Meleager thrust his horse between them and grasped their arms, squeezing them until they felt their elbows cracking in his iron hands.

"Listen to me," he whispered. "One more word out of you, and I will call off this hunt, send our guests home, and Atlanta and I will hunt the boar alone, as we have always wanted to do. But first I will smash your heads together just to show our guests where the fault lies."

The uncles said no more. Meleager sounded a call upon his horn that rang through the hills, and the glittering company rode out to find the boar.

They did not have far to ride. Their quarry came to meet them, taking up its position as wisely as a general disposing troops; it came to earth in a canyon where the walls narrowed so that it could be attacked only from the front, and by only two men at a time. This rocky bottleneck was overgrown with willows, and the boar crouched in there unseen, waiting for the hunters.

However, the hunters were old hands at this. They did not rush in to attack him, but strung themselves out before the entrance to his lair, shouting, clashing spear on shield, trying to taunt him into the open. They succeeded only too well, not knowing his size and speed. The boar came hurtling out of the willow brush with the crashing force of a huge boulder falling down a mountainside. He ploughed into a party of hunters, knocking them in all directions, whirling his huge bulk lightly as a fox, and cutting two of the men to shreds under his razor-sharp hooves. He charged again at the fleeing hunters, lunging at one with his tusks, and shearing his leg off at the hip.

The two warrior brothers, Telamon and Peleus, who became the father of Achilles, showed their great courage by walking slowly in on the boar, spears outthrust. Their attack inspired two of the others, Ancaeus and Eurytion, to walk in behind the boar from opposite sides. But the beast broke out of the circle of spears by charging Telamon. Peleus flung his spear; it grazed the boar's shoulder, was deflected, and pierced Eurytion, who fell dead. Now Ancaeus, swinging his battle-ax at the boar, had his thrust parried by a sweep of one tusk; and then with a counter-thrust the boar ripped out the man's belly, gutting him as a fisherman does a fish. The beast then whirled and charged Peleus, who might have died on the spot, leaving no son named Achilles (and Hector might have gone unslain, and Troy, perhaps, might have stood unburned), but Atalanta drew her bow and sent a shaft into the vulnerable spot behind the boar's ear. It sank in up to the feathers. Another beast would have been killed instantly, but the boar still lived and remained murderously strong.

Screaming with pain the boar chased Atalanta. Theseus rose from behind a rock and flung a javelin; he missed. Atalanta swiftly notched another arrow and stood facing the beast as it hurtled toward her. There was just enough time for her to send the shaft into his eye.

But Meleager, shouting a wild war-cry, flung himself in the boar's path, hurling a javelin as he ran. It went into the boar under his shoulder, turning him from his charge toward Meleager, who kept running, and leaped clear over the charging beast like a Cretan bull-dancer. He came down on the other side, and before the animal could turn, thrust his sword under the great hump of muscle, cutting the spinal cord and breaking the cable of hot life; the boar fell dead.

Meleager pulled out his sword, and then calmly as though on a stag-hunt, knelt at the side of the giant beast and skinned him. He walked to Atalanta with the bloody pelt in his arms, bowed, and offered it to her, saying, "Your arrow struck him first. The pelt belongs to you."

Now this boarhide was a most valuable present. It was so thick and tough that it made a wonderful flexible war vest, lighter and stronger than armor, able to turn spearthrust and flying arrow. There was much resentment when Meleager gave the hide to the girl; the uncles, seeing this resentment, reproached Meleager again, accusing him of favoritism and inhospitality. The elder uncle, Plexippus, began to curse Atalanta, calling her by filthy names; his brother echoed him.

Meleager wiped the blood from his sword and carefully dried it with a handful of rushes. He inspected the gleaming blade, and then swung it twice; the heads of his uncles rolled in the dust so swiftly severed that they still seemed to be cursing as they fell. Then Meleager said, "I beg you, sirs, pardon this unseemly family brawl; but if any one of you feels too much offended, I shall be glad to measure swords with him. If not, you are all invited to the castle, to a feast celebrating the death of the boar, and honoring his fair executioner, the huntress, Atalanta, whom I intend to make my wife."

The heroes raised a great shout. Many of them were still angry, others jealous, but they all admired courage when they saw it; besides they had had enough fighting for the day so they rode back to the castle, and Atalanta and Meleager rode off to be alone for a few hours before the feast.

When the hunters returned to the castle, they were met by the king and queen who eagerly demanded to hear their tale. But when they were told of the dispute over the hide and of how Meleager had killed his uncles and presented Atalanta to the company as his bride, the queen grew white with fury and rushed to her room.

There she sank to her knees on the stone floor and cried, "Bad prince, disobedient son, you have dispatched my two brothers to Tartarus, and in their noble stead propose to bring home this wild nameless nymph of the hills. This shall not be, my son, my enemy. The Fates have given your mother the power to end your evil ways . . ."

Mad with grief, Althaea sprang to the chest, flung it open, pulled the charred stick from its hiding place, and threw it on the fire. She watched it burn.

At this time Meleager and Atalanta were in their favorite place under the twisted olive tree on the cliff, looking out into the great blue gulf of space and speaking softly.

"I want to be your wife," said Atalanta. "You are the only one I shall ever love, but why must we live in a castle? Why must I be a queen, and wear dresses, and sit on a throne? Why can't we stay as we are, roaming the hills, hunting, fighting?"

"We will, we will!" cried Meleager. "For every day we spend indoors being king and queen and making laws and such, for each day spent so poorly, we will spend ten days riding, hunting, fighting, you and I together side by side. I promise you, Atalanta. And this I promise too . . ."

He stopped. She saw him clutch at his chest, saw his eyes bulge, his face blacken. She caught him in her arms. His head snapped back; his scorched lips parted. He uttered a strangling howl of agony; his head lolled, and he was dead.

In the castle, Queen Althaea prodded the fire with her toe, scattering the last ashes. Then she straightened her robes and went down to tend to her guests.

THE RACE

After Meleager's death, Calydon became hateful to Atalanta. She left its familiar crags and slopes, and made her way to Arcadia. Obeying some dim instinct, a dumb homeward impulse that was the only thing she felt in her terrible grief, she went back to Arcadia where she had been born.

The king, her father, now very old, realized from her story that she was his daughter, whom, as an infant, he had exposed on the mountain ... and that she had grown up to be as mighty a hunter and warrior as any son he could have hoped for. He recognized her as his child, and she lived in the castle.

But hunting was hateful to Atalanta now, and everything that reminded her of her murdered lover. Her fame had spread throughout the land, and the heroes who had gone on the Calydonian Hunt, and others too, came to woo the warrior-maiden for she was an orphan no more, but a princess who would inherit land and cattle and gold. So they came a-courting.

Atalanta could not bear the sight of them. "I will never marry another," she said to her father. "That part of me died with Meleager. I will never love another man. Send them away."

"I cannot insult them," said her father. "They are too powerful. If I seek to drive them away, they will make war upon me, conquer me; and you will be dragged off, a captive instead of a wife."

"Whoever takes me captive won't live long enough to enjoy it," said Atalanta. "However, let us do this: announce to them that I will marry only the man who can outrun me in a foot race. If he wins, he marries me; if he loses, he loses his head."

The king agreed. Atalanta's terms were announced. Most of the heroes who had watched her in action on the hunt, had observed her speed of movement, and had studied her long legs, knew what the outcome of a race must be, and decided to seek brides elsewhere. But some of the younger men were rash enough to persist. One by one, they raced Atalanta. The entire court turned out to see these races. Race followed race; she wanted no rest in between, and it seemed to the spectators that the young men still scrambled at the starting post as Atalanta flashed across the finish line.

She was merciless about imposing the penalty. Each losing suitor walked to the chopping block and paid with his head. Now, there was one young man, Hippomenes, who had also been at the Calydonian Hunt, although he had played no great role there. But he had fallen violently in love with Atalanta, so much in love that he was grieved at the death of Meleager because he knew that it would pain her so. Without ever being bold enough to make himself known to her, he had followed her at a distance, trailing her from Calydon to Arcadia and taking up residence there. He planned each day so that he would get a glimpse of her and this was enough to carry him to the next day. Still she had never met him.

When the races were announced, Hippomenes experienced a curious mixture of feelings. He was happy, on the one hand, that she was showing her scorn of other suitors; sad, on the other hand, because he realized that her scorn would extend to himself, if she knew him. He went each day to watch the races and again felt confused for he became each young man in the race and felt death crawl in his veins as he saw her flash across the finish line. He was each young man who laid his head on the bloody block, yet he was glad when the head rolled because there was one more rival gone. And through it all ran a curious thread of bitter joy, for his torment, he knew, had to end soon. The race would give him the chance to pay for this terrible love with his life.

When all the suitors had been beheaded, he announced himself as an entry. Everyone pleaded with him not to run. He was a gentle young man, with a soft voice and an easy smile. He did not look much like anyone's idea of a hero, and no one believed he had a chance. Even cruel Atalanta said, "Don't be a fool. Go lose your head over some other girl. I'm not for you."

But for all his gentleness, he could not be moved. He insisted so the race was set. Now, all the other young men who had raced Atalanta had prayed to various gods to give them victory: to Hermes, the wing-footed, god of games; to Ares, god of victories; to Artemis, mistress of the chase. They prayed to Athene for strategy, to Zeus, for strength. But Hippomenes prayed to none of these. He thought to himself, "The others want to coerce her. I want her to want me." . . . So he prayed to Aphrodite, goddess of love.

Aphrodite appeared to him when he was asleep, gave him three golden apples, and told him how to use them. When he awoke he knew that he had been dreaming, but there were the three golden apples gleaming on his bed. He hid them in his tunic and went out to race.

It was a brilliant sunny day; all the court was there. Atalanta had never appeared more beautiful than she looked that day walking to the starting post in her short white tunic, her long dark hair falling free. Hippomenes smiled at her and wished her good morning, holding tight to the slippery golden apples under his tunic so that they would not roll away before the race began. She received his greeting, and nodded, gravely. Then she studied him, frowning. Why was he clutching at his clothes in that odd way? That was no way to hold yourself before a race.

She felt a strange, hot lump form at the base of her throat; something about his hands, something terrible about the pose of those hands grasping at his tunic. Then she remembered, remembered the way her beloved Meleager had clutched at his belly when the curse was burning in him, just before he died in her arms.

She was so sunk in memory that she did not hear the trumpet call, starting the race, and Hippomenes was far in the lead when she woke up and began to run. He heard her light footfalls behind him, heard the easy music of her breathing. Then a great shout from the crowd, and he knew that she had closed the gap. He let one of the golden apples slip away and roll across her path.

And Atalanta, still remembering, running in a dream, saw the golden flash and automatically stooped to scoop up the rolling apple. She loped along slowly as she examined the glittering thing. She saw her face in it, distorted, made gross, and she thought, "That's how I will look when I am old . . ."

Then she heard the crowd shout, raised her head, and saw Hippomenes far in the lead. She darkened her mind, and let the speed surge through her legs and into her drumming feet until she was running just behind him again.

"Poor boy," she thought. "Am I tormenting him with hope? Or is such torture love's gift too? Would it have been better never to have seen Meleager, never to have loved him, never to have suffered by losing him? No! Worse, worse, worse!"

Just then Hippomenes dropped the second apple. It rolled, flashing.

"What a pretty thing," she thought. "Like one of Aphrodite's apples from that magic tree in the Hesperides. I will take it and the other one and bring them both to Calydon, to Meleager's grave."

Now Hippomenes had thrown this apple harder; it had rolled quite a way before she decided to go back for it. When she had picked it up, she saw Hippomenes far up the track, almost at the finish line. She ran with desperate speed then and caught him just two steps before the end.

He dropped the third apple. She laughed with scorn. "The fool . . . does he think I'll stop for that one and let him win? I'll simply cross the finish line and come back for the apple while he's being led to the block."

The apple lay before her feet. It was not rolling. All she had to do was bend in her course and scoop it up. But did she have time? The apple burned. It became a head bright with blood. Hippomenes' head falling under the ax. It changed into the head of Meleager's uncle being scythed off by the flashing sword . . . became Meleager's face bright with sweat and agony . . . became her own face, reflected, gross, distorted, old . . . growing now, swelling, blown up by the roaring of the crowd, mushrooming into the golden radiance of the sun—so enormous, so indifferently hot—touching the earth with seasons, budding flowers, beasts, hunters, nymphs, horses, amorous princes, angry queens . . . birth and murder. . . .

She held the three golden apples, dreaming into their polished fire, her face wet with tears, and the roaring of the crowd was dim, lost thunder, like the pounding of the surf. She stood there on the course, lost in her dream, as Hippomenes crossed the finish line and came back to claim his prize.

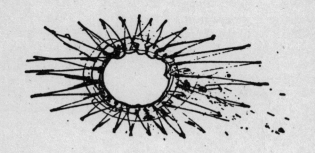

FABLES

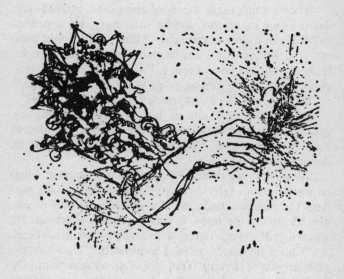

Midas

There was a king named Midas, and what he loved best in the world was gold. He had plenty of his own, but he could not bear the thought of anyone else having any. Each morning he awoke very early to watch the sunrise and said, "Of all the gods, if gods there be, I like you least, Apollo. How dare you ride so unthriftily in your sun-chariot scattering golden sheaves of light on rich and poor alike—on king and peasant, on merchant, shepherd, warrior? This is an evil thing, oh wastrel god, for only kings' should have gold; only the rich know what to do with it."

After a while these words of complaint, uttered each dawn, came to Apollo, and he was angry. He appeared to Midas in a dream and said, "Other gods would punish you, Midas, but I am famous for my even temper. Instead of doing you violence, I will show you how gracious I can be by granting you a wish. What is it to be?"

Midas cried, "Let everything I touch turn to gold!"

He shouted this out of his sleep in a strangling greedy voice, and the guards in the doorway nodded to each other and said, "The king calls out. He must be dreaming of gold again."

Wearied by the dream, Midas slept past sunrise; when he awoke it was full morning. He went out into his garden. The sun was high, the sky was blue. A soft breeze played among the trees. It was a glorious morning. He was still half asleep. Tatters of the dream were in his head.

"Can it be true?" he said to himself. "They say the gods appear in dreams. That's how men know them. On the other hand I know that dreams are false, teasing things. You can't believe them. Let us put it to the test."

He reached out his hand and touched a rose. It turned to gold—petals and stalk, it turned to gold and stood there rigid, heavy, gleaming. A bee buzzed out of its stiff folds, furious; it lit on Midas' hand to sting him. The king looked at the heavy golden bee on the back of his hand and moved it to his finger.

"I shall wear it as a ring," he said.

Midas went about touching all his roses, seeing them stiffen and gleam. They lost their odor. The disappointed bees rose in swarms and buzzed angrily away. Butterflies departed. The hard flowers tinkled like little bells when the breeze moved among them, and the king was well pleased.

His little daughter, the princess, who had been playing in the garden, ran to him and said, "Father, Father, what has happened to the roses?"

"Are they not pretty, my dear?"

"No! They're ugly! They're horrid and sharp and I can't smell them anymore. What happened?"

"A magical thing."

"Who did the magic?

"I did."

"Unmagic it, then! I hate these roses."

She began to cry.

"Don't cry," he said, stroking her head. "Stop crying, and I will give you a golden doll with a gold-leaf dress and tiny golden shoes."

She stopped crying. He felt the hair grow spiky under his fingers. Her eyes stiffened and froze into place. The little blue vein in her neck stopped pulsing. She was a statue, a figure of pale gold standing in the garden path with lifted face. Her tears were tiny golden beads on her golden cheeks. He looked at her and said, "This is unfortunate. I'm sorry it happened. I have no time to be sad this morning. I shall be busy turning things into gold. But, when I have a moment, I shall think about this problem; I promise." He hurried out of the garden which had become unpleasant to him.

On Midas' way back to the castle he amused himself by kicking up gravel in the path and watching it tinkle down as tiny nuggets. The door he opened became golden; the chair he sat upon became solid gold like his throne. The plates turned into gold, and the cups became gold cups before the amazed eyes of the servants, whom he was careful not to touch. He wanted them to continue being able to serve him; he was very hungry.

With great relish Midas picked up a piece of bread and honey. His teeth bit metal; his mouth was full of metal. He felt himself choking. He reached into his

mouth and pulled out a golden slab of bread, all bloody
now, and flung it through the window. Very lightly now
he touched the other food to see what would happen.
Meat . . . apples . . . walnuts . . . they all turned to gold
even when he touched them with only the tip of his finger . . . and when he did not touch them with his fingers, when he lifted them on his fork, they became gold
as soon as they touched his lips, and he had to put them
back onto the plate. He was savagely hungry. Worse
than hunger, when he thought about drinking, he realized that wine, or water, or milk would turn to gold in
his mouth and choke him if he drank. As he thought that
he could not drink, thirst began to burn in his belly. He
felt himself full of hot dry sand, felt that the lining of
his head was on fire.

"What good is all my gold?" he cried, "if I cannot
eat and cannot drink?"

He shrieked with rage, pounded on the table, and
flung the plates about. All the servants ran from the
room in fright. Then Midas raced out of the castle,
across the bridge that spanned the moat, along the
golden gravel path into the garden where the stiff flowers chimed hatefully, and the statue of his daughter
looked at him with scooped and empty eyes. There in
the garden, in the blaze of the sun, he raised his arms
heavenward, and cried, "You, Apollo, false god, traitor!
You pretended to forgive me, but you punished me with
a gift!"

Then it seemed to him that the sun grew brighter,
that the light thickened, that the sun-god stood before
him in the path, tall, stern, clad in burning gold. A voice
said, "On your knees, wretch!"

He fell to his knees.

"Do you repent?"

"I repent. I will never desire gold again. I will never
accuse the gods. Pray, revoke the fatal wish."

Apollo reached his hand and touched the roses. The tinkling stopped, they softened, swayed, blushed. Fragrance grew on the air. The bees returned, and the butterflies. He touched the statue's cheek. She lost her stiffness, her metallic gleam. She ran to the roses, knelt among them, and cried, "Oh, thank you, Father. You've changed them back again." Then she ran off, shouting and laughing.

Apollo said, "I take back my gift. I remove the golden taint from your touch, but you are not to escape without punishment. Because you have been the most foolish of men, you shall wear always a pair of donkey's ears."

Midas touched his ears. They were long and furry. He said, "I thank you for your forgiveness, Apollo . . . even though it comes with a punishment."

"Go now," said Apollo. "Eat and drink. Enjoy the roses. Watch your child grow. Life is the only wealth, man. In your great thrift, you have been wasteful of life, and that is the sign you wear on your head. Farewell."

Midas put a tall pointed hat on his head so that no one would see his ears. Then he went in to eat and drink his fill.

For years he wore the cap so that no one would know of his disgrace. But the servant who cut his hair had to know so Midas swore him to secrecy, warning that it would cost him his head if he spoke of the king's ears. But the servant who was a coward was also a gossip. He could not bear to keep a secret, especially a secret so mischievous. Although he was afraid to tell it, he felt that he would burst if he didn't.

One night he went out to the banks of the river, dug a little hole, put his mouth to it, and whispered, "Midas has donkey's ears, Midas has donkey's ears . . ." and quickly filled up the hole again, and ran back to the castle, feeling better.

But the river-reeds heard him, and they always whisper to each other when the wind seethes among them. They were heard whispering, "Midas has donkey's ears . . . donkey's ears . . ." and soon the whole country was whispering, "Have you heard about Midas? Have you heard about his ears?"

When the king heard, he knew who had told the secret and ordered the man's head cut off; but then he thought, "The god forgave me, perhaps I had better forgive this blabbermouth." Therefore he let the treacherous man keep his head.

Then Apollo appeared again and said, "Midas, you have learned the final lesson, mercy. As you have done, so shall you be done by."

And Midas felt his long hairy ears dwindling back to normal.

He was an old man now. His daughter, the princess, was grown. He had grandchildren. Sometimes he tells his smallest granddaughter the story of how her mother was turned into a golden statue, and he says, "See, I'm changing you too. Look, your hair is all gold."

And she pretends to be frightened.

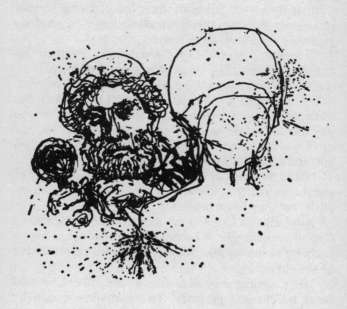

Pygmalion

The women of Cyprus were displeased with Pygmalion. He was one of the few unmarried young men on the island, and it seemed that he meant to stay that way. He was a sculptor who lived alone in a house he had knocked together out of an old stable, one enormous room on a hill overlooking the sea, far away from any neighbor. Here he spent the days very happily. Great unhewn blocks of marble stood about, and tubs of clay, and a crowd of figures, men and women, nymphs, satyrs, wolves, lions, bulls, and dolphins. Some of them were half-carved, some of them clay daubs, almost shapeless; and others were finished statues, marvelous gleaming shapes of white marble.

Sometimes people came and bought Pygmalion's figures. He sold only those he was tired of looking at, but would never set a price. He took anything offered. Often, he would give his work away, if he thought that someone enjoyed looking at it and had no money to pay. He ate when he was hungry, slept when he was tired, worked when he felt like it, swam in the sea when hot, and spent days without seeing anyone.

"Oh, I have plenty of company," he'd say. "Plenty of statues around, you know. Not very good conversationalists, but they listen beautifully."

Now, all this irritated the mothers and daughters of Cyprus exceedingly. A bachelor is bad enough, a happy bachelor is intolerable. And so they were resolved that he should marry.

"He's earning enough to keep a wife . . . or he would be if he charged properly. That's another reason he needs one. My Althea is a very shrewd girl. She'd see he got the right prices for his work . . ."

"My Laurel is an excellent housekeeper. She'd clean out that pig-sty of his, and make it fit to live in . . ."

"My daughter has very strict ideas. She'd make him toe the mark. Where does he get the models for those nymph statues? Tell me that? Who knows what goes on in that stable of his? . . ."

"*My* daughter . . ."

And so it went. They talked like this all the time, and Pygmalion was very much aware of their plans for him. More than ever he resolved to keep himself to himself.

Now Cyprus was an island sacred to Aphrodite, for it was the first land she touched when she arose from the sea. The mothers of the island decided to use her favor for their own purposes. They crowded into the temple of Aphrodite and recited this prayer:

"Oh, great goddess of Love, you who rose naked and dripping from the sea and walked upon this shore, making it blossom with trees and flowers, you, Aphrodite, hear our plea: touch the heart of young Pygmalion, who has become as hard as his own marble. Weave your amorous spell, plaiting it into the tresses of one of the maidens, making it a snare for his wild loneliness. Bid your son, the Archer of Love, plant one of his arrows in the indifferent young man so that he becomes infected with a sweet sickness for which there is only one cure. Please, goddess, forbid him all solitary joy. Bind him to one of our maidens. Make him love her and take her as his wife."

That night Pygmalion, dreaming, was visited by the goddess who said, "Pygmalion, I have been asked to marry you off. Do you have any preferences?"

Pygmalion, being an artist, was acquainted with the terrible reality of dreams and knew that the matter was serious, that he was being threatened. He said, "There is one lady I fancy. But she is already married."

"Who?"

"You."

"Me?"

"You, Aphrodite, queen of beauty, lady of delight. How can you think that I who in my daily work will accept nothing less than the forms of ideal beauty, how can you think that I could pin my highest aspiration on any but the most perfect face and form? Yours, Aphrodite. Yours, yours. I love you, and you alone. And until I can find a mortal maid of the same perfection, I will not love."

Now, Aphrodite, although a goddess, was also a woman. In fact, her divinity was precisely this, womanliness raised to its highest power. She was much pleased by this ardent praise. She knelt beside Pygmalion and, stroking his face, said, "Truly, you are a fair-spoken young man. I find your arguments very persuasive. But what am I to do? I have promised the mothers of Cyprus that you shall wed, and I must not break my promise."

"Did you tell them *when?*"

"No, I set no time."

"Then grant me this: permit me to remain unwed until I do one more statue. It will be my masterwork, the thing I have been training myself for. Let me do it now, and allow me to remain unmarried until I complete it for the vision is upon me, goddess. The time has come. I must do this last figure."

"Of whom?"

"Of you, of course! Of you, of you! I told you that I have loved you all my life without ever having seen you. And now that you have appeared to me, now that I do see you, why then I must carve you in marble. It is simple. This is what my life is for; it is my way of loving you, a way that you cannot deny me."

"I see . . . And how long will this work take?"

"Until it is finished. What else can I say? If you will be good enough to visit me like this whenever you can spare the time, I will fill my eyes with you and work on your image alone, putting all else aside. Once and for all I shall be able to cast in hard cold marble the flimsy, burning dream of man, his dream of beauty, his dream of you . . ."

"Very well," said Aphrodite, "you may postpone your marriage until my statue is completed." She smiled at him. "And every now and again I shall come to pose."

Pygmalion worked first in clay. He took it between his hands and thought of Aphrodite—of her round arms, of the strong column of her neck, of her long, full thighs, of the smooth swimming of her back muscles when she turned from the waist—and his hands followed his thinking, pressing the clay to the shape of her body. She came to him at night, sliding in and out of his dreams, telling him stories about herself. He used a whole tubfull of clay making a hundred little Aphrodites, each in a different pose. He caught her at that moment when she emerged from the sea, shaking back her wet hair, lifting her face to the sky which she saw for the first time. He molded her in the Hall of the Gods receiving marriage offers, listening to Poseidon, and Hermes, and Apollo press their claims, head tilted, shoulders straight, smiling to herself, pleasing everyone, but refusing to answer. He molded her in full magnificent fury, punishing Narcissus, kneeling on the grass, teasing the shy Adonis, and then mourning him, slain.

He caught her in a hundred poses, then stood the little clay figures about, studying them, trying to mold them in his mind to a total image that he could carve in marble. He had planned to work slowly. After all, the whole thing was a trick of his to postpone marriage; but as he made the lovely little dolls and posed them among her adventures, his hands took on a schedule of their own. The dream invaded daylight, and he found himself working with wild fury.

When the clay figures were done, he was ready for marble. He set the heavy mass of polished stone in the center of the room and arranged his clay studies about it. Then he took mallet and chisel, and began to work— it was as if the cold tools became living parts of himself. The chisel was like his own finger, with a sharp fingernail edge; the mallet was his other hand, curled into a fist. With these living tools he reached into the marble and worked the stone as if it were clay, chopping, stroking, carving, polishing. And from the stone a body began to rise as Aphrodite had risen from the white foam of the sea.

He never knew when he had finished. He had not eaten for three days. His brain was on fire, his hands flying. He had finished carving; he was polishing the marble girl now with delicate files. Then, suddenly, he knew that it was finished. His head felt full of ashes; his hands hung like lumps of meat. He fell onto his pallet and was drowned in sleep.

He awoke in the middle of the night. The goddess was standing near his bed, he saw. Had she come to pose for him again? It was too late. Then he saw that it was not Aphrodite, but the marble figure standing in the center of the room, the white marble gathering all the moonlight to her. She shone in the darkness, looking as though she were trying to leap from the pediment.

He went to the statue and tried to find something unfinished, a spot he could work on. But there was nothing. She was complete. Perfect. A masterwork. Every line of her drawn taut by his own strength stretched to the breaking point, the curvings of her richly rounded with all the love he had never given to a human being. There she was, an image of Aphrodite. But not Aphrodite. She was herself, a marble girl, modeled after the goddess, but different; younger; human.

"You are Galatea," he said. "That is your name."

He went to a carved wooden box and took out jewels that had belonged to his mother. He decked Galatea in sapphires and diamonds. Then he sat at the foot of the statue, looking at it, until the sun came up. The birds sang, a donkey brayed; he heard the shouting of children, the barking of dogs. He sat there, looking at her. All that day he sat, and all that night. Still he had not eaten. And now it seemed that all the other marble figures in the room were swaying closer, were shadows crowding about, threatening him.

She did not move. She stood there, tall, radiant. His mother's jewels sparkled on her throat and on her arms. arble foot spurned the pediment.

Then Aphrodite herself stepped into the room. She said, "I have come to make you keep your promise, Pygmalion. You have finished the statue. You must marry."

"Whom?"

"Whomever you choose. Do you not wish to select your own bride?"

"Yes."

"Then choose. Choose any girl you like. Whoever she is, whatever she is, she shall love you. For I am pleased with the image you have made of me. Choose."

"I choose—her," said Pygmalion, pointing to the statue.

"You may not."

"Why not?"

"She does not live. She is a statue."

"My statues will outlive all who are living now," said Pygmalion.

"That is just a way of speaking. She is not flesh and blood; she is a marble image. You must choose a living girl."

"I must choose where I love. I love her who is made in your image, goddess."

"It cannot be.'

"You said, 'whoever she is, whatever she is . . .'"

"Yes, but I did not mean a statue."

"I did. You call her lifeless, but I say my blood went into her making. My bones shaped hers. My fingers loved her surfaces. I polished her with all my knowledge, all my wit. She has seen all my strength, all my weakness, she has watched me sleep, played with my dreams. We *are* wed, Aphrodite, in a fatal incomplete way. Please, dear goddess, give her to me."

"Impossible."

"You are a goddess. Nothing is impossible."

"I am the Goddess of Love. There is no love without life."

"There is no life without love. I know how you can do it. Look . . . I stand here. I place my arm about her; my face against hers. Now, use your power, turn me to marble too. We shall be frozen together in this moment of time, embracing each other through eternity. This will suffice. For I tell you that without her my brain is ash, my hands are meat; I do not wish to breathe, to see, to be."

Aphrodite, despite herself, was warmed by his pleas. After all, he had made the statue in her image. It was pleasing to know that her beauty, even cast in lifeless marble, could still drive a young man mad.

"You are mad," she said. "Quite mad. But in people like you, I suppose, it is called inspiration. Very well, young sir, put your arms about her again."

Pygmalion embraced the cold marble. He kissed the beautiful stiff lips, and then he felt the stone flush with warmth. He felt the hard polished marble turn to warm silky flesh. He felt the mouth grow warm and move against his. He felt arms come up and hug him tight. He was holding a live girl in his arms.

He stepped off the pediment, holding her hand. She stepped after him. They fell on their knees before Aphrodite and thanked her for her gift.

"Rise, beautiful ones," she said. "It is the morning of love. Go to my temple, adorn it with garlands. You, Pygmalion, set about the altar those clever little dolls of me you have made. Thank me loudly for my blessings for I fear the mothers of Cyprus will not be singing my praises so ardently for some time."

She left. Galatea looked about the great dusty studio, littered with tools, scraps of marble, and spillings of clay. She looked at Pygmalion—tousled, unshaven, with bloodshot eyes and stained tunic—and said, "Now, dear husband, it's my turn to work on you."

MYTHOLOGY BECOMES LANGUAGE

Many of the characters, events, and places of the Greek myths have entered the English language. It is interesting to see how these words have been derived from Greek tales, and how the names of gods, goddesses, heroes, and monsters have become a part of our everyday speech.

Aphrodisiac, a love-potion, was named for Aphrodite, goddess of love.

Arachne, meaning "spider" in Greek, was adopted to describe in science the spider family which includes scorpions, mites, and ticks: arachnida or arachnoidea. The adjective *arachnoid* means anything resembling a spider's web.

Athene was also known as Pallas Athene. Pallas signifies "brandisher," that is, as a spear. An asteroid was named Pallas as well as a very rare metallic element called palladium which was named after the asteroid. Because a statue of Pallas Athene which stood in front of the city of Troy was supposed to have helped preserve the city from danger, the word *palladium* also has come to mean a potent safeguard.

Atlas, a map, was named after the Titan who bore the sky on his shoulders and was turned to stone by Perseus.

Calliope is the name of a musical instrument. The mother of Orpheus was named Calliope because she was the Muse of Eloquence and Heroic Poetry. The name comes from two words meaning "beauty" and "voice."

Cloth is a plain little word with a very dramatic history. The Greeks believed that destiny was controlled by three terrible sisters called the Fates. Clotho spun the thread of life on her spindle; Lachesis measured the thread; and the most dangerous sister, Atropos, Lady of the Shears, snipped the thread of life when it had been measured out. Our word *cloth* comes from Clotho, the spinner.

Cronos refers to the god of time. From this word we have the noun *chronology* which describes an arrangement of events in order of occurrence. *Chronic* describes something that continues over a long period of time. A chronicler is one who records a historical account of events in the order of time. A timepiece of great accuracy is called a chronometer.

Cyclops, plural **Cyclopes,** is derived from two Greek words meaning "circle" and "eye." We have adopted *cyclops* in the field of biology to describe the group of tiny, free-swimming crustaceans which have a single eye. *Cyclopic* is an adjective meaning monstrous; *cyclopia* is a noun used for a massive abnormality in which the eyes are partly or wholly fused. The word has been used as a root to describe a wheel in such words as tricycle, bicycle, and motorcycle. It is used to describe a violent storm which moves in a circle: cyclone. It also appears in the word encyclopedia to describe circular (or complete) learning. A cyclotron is a large apparatus used for the multiple acceleration of ions to very high speeds.

Echo is derived from the name of the nymph *Echo*, who fell in love with Narcissus. She could not tell him of her love because she was under a curse which allowed her to repeat only the last word of what was said to her.

Elysian Fields, which means a "place of great happiness," inspired the French to call their famous boulevard in Paris the Champs Elysées.

Erinyes, or the Furies, punished people for their crimes on the earth. They were called the Eumenides, which meant "the kindly ones." This name reveals the Greek habit of calling unpleasant things by pleasant names. We use the word *euphemism* to describe words which do not say the unpleasant idea intended.

Erotic, relating to love, is derived from *Eros*, Aphrodite's son, the secret archer, whose arrows were tipped with the sweet poison of love.

Fortune is a very common word that is derived from *Fortuna*, the Roman goddess of luck and vengeance, mistress of destiny. Actually, her name was a variant of the Latin word, *vortumna*, meaning "turner," because she turned the giant wheel of the year, stopping it at either happiness, sorrow, life, or death.

Galatea was the name of the statue which Pygmalion carved to the shape of his heart's desire.

Hades is used today to describe the home of the dead. Hades comes from the Greek word meaning "the unseen." Hades was also known in Roman mythology as Pluto, the god of wealth—from the Greek word *plutus*, meaning "wealth." We use the word *plutocracy* to describe a government run by wealthy people.

Icarian, meaning "of bold, vaulting ambition," is derived from Icarus, son of Daedalus, who insisted on flying too near the sun and died doing it.

Jove, one of the names for Jupiter and Zeus, has come to mean "born under a lucky planet and therefore happy and healthy." The adjective *jovial*, and the noun *joviality* all derive from the word *Jove*. We even hear the expression, "By Jove." The planet Jupiter is the largest body in the solar system except the sun.

Junoesque, meaning stately, majestic, is a word used to describe women only and comes from Juno, the Roman Queen of Heaven, who was of imposing figure.

Labyrinth, a "maze," is derived from the name of the prison-garden full of puzzling paths, built by Daedalus at King Minos' command to confine the Minotaur. Actually, the Cretan word, *labys*, means "ax"; the double-headed ax was the royal symbol in Crete. The palace of the king at Knossos was known as the "Ax-House," and it was in the garden of this palace that Daedalus built his maze.

Martial, meaning "warlike," comes from Mars, the Roman god of war.

Medusa locks, meaning "wild hair," is a phrase named after the hissing snake coiffure of the fearsome Gorgon sister, Medusa, whom Perseus killed.

Mercurial, meaning "swift, unstable, changeable," refers to the disposition of Mercury, the Roman messenger-god.

Midas touch, the golden touch, is said of those who are good at making money.

Muses refers to the nine goddesses of dancing, poetry and astronomy. We use the verb *muse* to describe the act of pondering or meditating. The words *music, musician* and *musical* all come from this word.

Narcissistic means to be obsessed by the idea of one's own beauty. It is taken from *Narcissus,* the boy who fell in love with his own reflection in a stream and knelt there admiring it until he became rooted to the ground and was changed into a flower.

Narcissus is the name of a family of flowers which includes daffodils and jonquils. The word *narcissist* is a psychological term meaning a person who loves himself.

Neptune, the Roman god of the sea, has given his name to countless restaurants and inns, especially those emphasizing sea food.

Olympus was the home of the Greek gods. The term has come to mean something which is grand, imposing, or heavenly. The great festival of games was called Olympian Games and today we call the world-famous athletic contest the Olympics.

Oracle is derived from the Greek word meaning "to pray." It is used to refer to places where people pray: oratories; to great speakers: orators; and even great speeches: orations. A person who seems to possess great knowledge or intuition is called an oracle, and his statements are described as oracular.

Orpheum refers to Orpheus, the sweetest singer to ever sing. This term is used by many theaters and places of entertainment.

Pandora has the same prefix as Pantheon and means, of course, all. The root *doron* is a Greek word for gift; therefore, Pandora was all-gifted.

Panic is derived from the god *Pan*, the goat-footed, flute-playing king of field and wood whose war cry was supposed to spread frenzy and fear among his enemies.

Pantheon is made up of two Greek words: *pan* meaning "all," and *theos* meaning "god," or "having something to do with gods." The prefix *pan* is used in such words as panacea, Panama, and even Pan American. The root *theos* is used in such words as theology and theocracy.

Procrustes bed is a phrase meaning any difficult situation which cannot be changed but to which man must adapt himself. It comes from the uncomfortable hospitality offered by the innkeeper Procrustes, who bolted guests to the bed. If they were too short, he stretched them; if too long, he chopped off their legs to fit. However, Theseus made him lie in his own bed.

Prometheus means "forethinker." It has come to mean something that is life-giving, daringly original, or creative. An element which is a fission product of uranium is called promethium. The prefix *pro* is used in countless words today.

Psyche is perhaps the most misused word in the language. In Greek it meant "soul" and was personified in myth by a beautiful princess, beloved of Eros himself, who lost her husband and her sense of herself through mistrust but regained both when she dropped her suspicions and took on the risks that love brings. In English, however, the word has come to mean the entire mental apparatus and has given birth to a host of words like psychotic, psychology, psychoanalysis, etc.

Pygmalion, the term applied to a man who can train a girl to be the way he wants, is derived from Pygmalion, the sculptor of Cyprus, who carved a statue in the shape of his heart's desire.

Python, which comes from the Greek word "to rot," is used to describe snakes such as the boa which kill its prey by crushing it. The adjective *pythogenic* is used to describe something which is produced by putrefaction or filth.

Saturday is named for the god Saturn, a Roman name for Cronos.

Stygian comes from the river Styx. It has come to be used when describing anything from the underworld. Stygian darkness is a favorite expression of poets.

Terpsichorean, relating to the dance, is derived from the Muse, Terpsichore, who presided over dance.

Titan, which referred to the race of giants, has been used to describe anything which is enormous in size or strength. The famous ship which sank when it hit an iceberg was called the *Titanic*.

Typhoon, a violent wind, comes from Typhon, a terrible monster. He was half donkey, half serpent; he had great leathery wings and flew through the air shrieking horribly, spitting flames.

Vestal means nunlike. The term is derived from Vesta, the Roman goddess of the hearth. In ancient Rome, maidens were consecrated to the service of this goddess; their duty was to keep the sacred flame burning upon her altar night and day. They lived in her temple always and never married.

Volcano is derived from Vulcan, the Roman smith-god, who took a mountain as his smithy. When he heated up his forge, clouds of smoke arose from the mountain.

RECOMMENDED READING

Asimov, Isaac. *Words from the Myths*. Houghton Mifflin: Boston, 1961.

Bulfinch, Thomas. *Bulfinch's Mythology*. Thomas Y. Crowell: New York (no date).

Grant, Michael. *Myths of the Greeks and Romans*. World Publishers: New York, 1962.

Graves, Robert. *The Greek Myths*. Penguin Books: Baltimore, 1955.

Hamilton, Edith. *Mythology*. New American Library: New York, 1940.

Hamilton, Edith. *The Greek Way to Western Civilization*. New American Library: New York, 1948.

Hays, H. R. *In the Beginnings*. G. P. Putnam's Sons: New York, 1963.

Rose, H. J. *A Handbook of Greek Mythology*. E. P. Dutton: New York, 1959.

Schwab, Gustav. *Gods and Heroes: Myths and Epics of Ancient Greece*. Fawcett World Library: New York, 1965.

Updike, John. *The Centaur*. Knopf: New York, 1963.

ABOUT THE AUTHOR

BERNARD EVSLIN is a novelist, playwright, film writer and director. He has had several plays produced, both on and off Broadway, among them *The Geranium Hat*. His novel, *Merchants of Venus*, was published in 1964.